Jamie Turner grew up in W_ _ _ Sussex and is currently studying his first year of A-levels before deciding on university places for 2024/2025.

Jamie currently lives with his mother, stepfather and two dogs.

When not studying, Jamie focuses his time and energy on his two passions in life: playing basketball and writing novels and screenplays. Jamie's first novel, *When A Man Becomes A Monster*, is an immersive read with a fascinating cast of characters.

You can expect to see many novels and screenplays in the future from this bright and aspiring young author. Jamie is currently represented by Austin Macauley Publishers.

I would like to dedicate this book to my nan, Barbara Fowles who constantly read my stories and gave me feedback and encouragement. Without her, none of this would be possible.

Jamie Turner

WHEN A MAN BECOMES A MONSTER

When he has lost all hope, all object in life, man becomes a monster in his misery.

AUSTIN MACAULEY PUBLISHERS™

LONDON • CAMBRIDGE • NEW YORK • SHARJAH

A CIP catalogue record for this title is available from the British Library.

ISBN 9781035833757 (Paperback)
ISBN 9781035833764 (ePub e-book)

www.austinmacauley.com

First Published 2023
Austin Macauley Publishers Ltd®
1 Canada Square
Canary Wharf
London
E14 5AA

I would like to thank my mother, Joanne Rowe and step-father, Simon Rowe for their continued support in everything I do and Austin Macauley Publishers for providing me with the opportunity to bring my book to life and share it with a wide audience. Without you, none of this would be possible.

Chapter 1

When he lost all hope, all objects in life, man becomes a monster in his misery.

Within a hospital room, there was a birth taking place. There was a man, the father, and a woman, the mother giving birth to a child. Doctors surrounded the mother as she screamed in agony. The father held her hand and said, "It's OK. It's OK, darling. I'm here. Just keep pushing."

"The baby is coming; just one last push," the doctor said, and with one final scream, the baby was born as the doctor took the child wrapping him into a towel as he handed the child to the mother. The mother began to cry as the husband gets closer.

"Oh, he's beautiful. Thank you, doctor," he said.

"So have we got a name for the little devil?" the doctor asked.

"Yes, his name is Jason… Jason Mitchells," the mother crying in joy responded.

The doctor smiled, "Congratulations, and welcome to the world, little Jason. I'll leave you two to it."

12 Years Later

A boy headed down the stairs of his home where the same couple was sitting at a breakfast table; the child joined them.

"Morning, son. How did you sleep?" the father asked.

"The same as the night before and the one before that," the boy replied.

"A bit grumpy today, aren't we?" the dad replied.

"Oh, Richard, leave Jason alone. He's just woken up," the mother said.

"OK OK. Just trying to make conversation," responded Richard.

The mother placed breakfast in front of Jason and Richard.

"Beans and egg again? What a surprise!" said Jason.

"Don't speak to your mother like that, Jason. Apologise this instant," Richard said in frustration.

"Sorry, but I'm not hungry," Jason answered as he stormed off grabbing his bag and headed to school.

Richard yelled out to him as he left, "Hey, Jason, get—"

But the mother stopped him. "Let him go, Richard. He just needs space," she said as she held Richard.

"I do worry about him. He just doesn't seem to fit in with anyone," Richard responded.

"Just give him time. Everyone's different, honey. Now eat your food. It is getting cold," the mother responded as she walked off.

"Yeah, I'm sure you're right. I'm sure he'll be alright," Richard mumbled.

Jason was walking through the woods by himself talking to himself.

"They just don't understand. All they do is sleep, eat, work and repeat. No difference. I won't fall in line. I won't join everyone in an endless cycle of repetition. I'm... I'm gonna make a name for myself do something different and be remembered for something. Yeah, I'm gonna break the cycle and be better and…"

Suddenly, three other children much bigger than Jason but of similar age appeared.

"Ohhhh… look, it's the freak. Hey, freak, you talking to your imaginary friends?" one of them said, and the other two laughed.

"Are you sure his imaginary friends even like him?" They all laughed again.

"Leave me alone, Marcus," Jason responded.

"What you say, freak, you talking back to me. You wouldn't want a repeat of last week now, would you?" Marcus responded angrily.

"You act all tough, but in the end, you are just as weak as everyone else," Jason spat at Marcus.

Marcus got angry.

"Oh, yeah, let's find out," he yelled as all of them chased Jason. Jason sprinted at full speed jumping and ducking through the woods. The others closely followed, he heard them shouting at him, shouting freak, loser and other insults. Jason finally tripped on a tree root on the ground and fell face down in the dirt. He screamed in pain as the bullies surrounded him.

"Now let's see who's really weak," Marcus said. All the three of them kicked and punched Jason as he wiggled on the ground in pain. They ripped his clothes and bruised his bones until they eventually stopped, and Marcus spat on Jason. "Who's weak now, huh?" He kicked him one last time. "Freak… he says… Let's go, guys. Leave the worm in the dirt."

They walked off all laughing and making fun of Jason as Jason struggled to move. Blood was dripping from his face, and a mixture of dirt and bruises covered his body. With his clothes partly ripped, he stumbled to his knees and stared at the tree root, which tripped him up.

Jason grabbed a sharp rock and screamed smashing the root with the rock again and again and again screaming until the root was completely ripped apart when Jason dropped down again laying on the floor in exhaustion crying. Then Jason rose to his feet, wiped away his tears and smiled as he put the sharp rock in his pocket and continued to walk.

Jason approached a makeshift house built from sticks, which he built himself.

"Finally, home, solitude," Jason said. He entered the stick house, which was covered in drawings of people dying that he had hand-drawn. Pictures displayed him murdering people.

When Jason sat down, he picked up a pencil and started drawing and said, "I will show them. I will show them all. Every last one of them will suffer. I will free them from their mediocre lives… their mediocre existence… starting with you," as Jason placed the new drawing in the centre of all the others with the person he was going to kill labelled Marcus.

Jason arrived at school; he had done his best to hide his injuries. He sat alone at the back of every class sitting there staring into nothing… not listening… not talking… barely even blinking until someone throws a paper ball at him. Jason shook out of his trance and opened it. It read 'FREAK'.

Jason looked up to see Marcus and his friends all laughing about it. Jason crushed the paper in his hands in pure anger as he pulled out his notebook and wrote in it. As the day progressed, Jason was lurking behind Marcus and his friends most of the day, his mind repeating the words.

"Dear diary, today has been just like any other. I woke up. I was given food. I went to school and sat through the pointless classes, and now I am about to head home, but today is going to be different.

"Today is the day I break the barrier of repetition, which everyone else follows so precisely. Today, I become something more. Today, I become different. Today, I kill Marcus Roller."

Jason followed Marcus and his friends through the forest and waited for them to leave him.

"You think that freak learnt his lesson this morning?" Marcus said. The other two laughed and chuckled.

"Yeah, but if he hasn't, we can always do it worse next time," one of them said. Marcus laughed.

"Right, I gotta go this way. Now my mum's expecting me back today," one of his friends said. The other nodded.

"Yeah, mine too."

"Alright, I'll see you guys tomorrow," Marcus said. They walked off.

"Yeah, see you tomorrow, Marcus," they replied.

"Oh no, you won't," Jason whispered. Jason continued to follow Marcus. When he stood on a twig, Marcus spun around and saw Jason.

"What the hell are you doing here, freak? Have you been following me? You a stalker now, huh?" Marcus said.

Jason threw off his bag and raised his fists to fight. Marcus surprised.

"Oh, so you want another beating? You're crazy," Marcus continued.

"Maybe," Jason spat onto the floor and replied, and they charged at each other. Jason threw an early swing and smacked Marcus in the chin causing him to stumble back. Marcus held his jaw.

"Oh, you're gonna pay for that, freak," he yelled. Marcus tackled Jason into a tree and repeatedly punched Jason in the stomach until Jason grabbed Marcus's ears and twisted them causing Marcus to let go of Jason and allowing him to kick Marcus in the stomach and punch him in the face.

Marcus stumbled back again, and Jason threw another punch, but Marcus blocked the punch deflecting Jason's arm and charged him to the floor and punched Jason in the face nearly a dozen times before standing back up. Jason moaned in pain on the floor while blood erupted from his mouth. Marcus looked down at him.

"It's almost like you like the pain. You're more than just a freak," he spoke.

Jason rose to his feet once again spitting blood onto Marcus's shirt.

"Maybe I do," he replied.

Jason charged at Marcus, but Marcus grabbed him and held him to his chest and squeezed him.

"How many bones do I have to break before you learn your lesson? You're nothing, freak. You're nobody. I bet no one even knows your name," said Marcus.

Jason's face crunched in anger, and he plunged his teeth into Marcus's neck. Blood flooded from his throat and from his mouth. Marcus let go of Jason and dropped to the ground in pain and fear and struggled to breathe. Jason stood over him and swallowed Marcus's blood and flesh.

"Hmmm… the taste of fear… is quite delicious. Marcus, dear Marcus, you've gotten it backwards. I am not the loser… the freak… the nobody… You are… you are the one who commits to conformity… who follows everyone else… Not me. I just hope you will be able to see… see what I become… see how I fix the world," Jason said as he pulled out the sharp rock from his pocket.

Marcus attempted to crawl away, but Jason knelt over him and plunged the rock into his head again and again and again as blood sprayed over him. Jason smashed Marcus's face in two before rising to his feet and staring down at the body.

He laughed, laughing so much, before finally stopping and saying, "I have done it. I have cured you, Marcus. Now you will not know the pain of living a life of repetition, a meaningless life.

"And ohhh… did it feel good, ha? You have awoken me. I now see who I am. I see what I am. I am no man destined to work a desk job. I am the next thing… the next villain… the next monster… The world manifested to tip the scales of peace, and I will not disappoint. I will burn it all down."

Jason placed the rock into his pocket and ripped off Marcus's shirt saying, "Can't have the police finding my blood. I've got so much more to do."

Jason ran into the woods taking the shirt and rock with him until eventually reaching his house. He climbed in through a window and washed off the blood from his clothes and replaced them, so his parents wouldn't see the rips. He then hid the rock and bloodied shirt under his bed, then climbed back out of the window and entered the house through the front door where his mother greeted him.

"How was school, honey?"

"It was good, mum. It was different," Jason answered with a sinister grin. Jason approached his father.

"Dad, do you think I could learn to fight?" he said.

"Well, look who's finally got a club. What type do you want to do, son? Karate? Judo? Boxing? Something else?" Richard asked.

"All of them. I would like to do all of them," Jason said.

Chapter 2

Six years had passed, and Jason turned 18 now, and he was fighting someone at a karate dojo. Jason perfectly dodged several kicks and swung from his opponent before kicking him in the knee causing his opponent to drop down to one knee. Jason spun and kicked his opponent in the face, knocking him out; the dojo sensei clapped.

"Another win for the champion. Anyone else up for the challenge?" The other students were sitting all trembling in fear as Jason stared at them all as the sensei said, "No? Well, Jason, you truly are my greatest student. It's a shame this will be our last session together. I will miss training you, my master piece. However, on a more happy note, have you made a decision on a college yet?"

"No, sensei. I think I might take a year off you know and take some personal time," Jason replied.

"Ah... I see. Planning on travelling? See the world?"

"Something like that," Jason replied.

Jason arrived home.

"How was the last session, son. You kick anyone's ass?" his dad Richard asked him.

"Richard, language..." the mother responded.

"Yeah, just as I always have," Jason said as he headed upstairs and entered his room. Everywhere, there were dozens of trophies for every martial art and fighting sport you can think of, as Jason placed his karate robes into a frame on the wall next to all his other uniforms saying, "I have done it. I have mastered every martial art, and now I can finally begin. Begin building my legacy of blood and fire."

He turned to a box and pulled out Marcus's old, blooded shirt and the blooded rock and said, "If only you were still here, Marcus, so I could show you what I am about to do. The past six years of painful repetition, all about to unfold... It will be beautiful." Jason laughed manically.

It's night when Jason climbed out of his window and headed to the park walking through the dark alleyways until finally reaching the park and seeing a group of drunks. There were three of them.

"Hello, my friends. I have a question for you all if you don't mind," Jason approached saying.

"What, ah sure kid?" one of the drunks said.

"Tell me, do you like life? Do you like your miserable pointless existence? Or would you like someone, something to end it all?" Jason added.

"What?" one of the drunks asked when Jason plunged a knife into the drunk's stomach. The drunk screamed in pain as Jason slid the dagger across the drunk's stomach disembowelling him. The other two stumbled to their feet in shock, standing there, frozen.

"Hey, you... you don't have to do this. You want the booze here. Here take it... take it," one said.

"Oh, you feeble-minded creature. I don't want the alcohol. I just want to watch you bleed," Jason said.

Suddenly, one of them threw a punch at Jason, but Jason dodged it grabbing the drunk and slitting his throat. Jason laughed, and he turned to the last drunk who threw his wallet at Jason.

"Here, take it... take it, please. Don't hurt me, please," said the drunk.

Jason placed his hand on the drunk's shoulder.

"Shhhh... shhh... don't be afraid. I am going to release you from pain, or then again maybe you should be afraid," Jason said as he impaled the drunk through the side of the head as his body dropped to the floor. Jason laughed saying, "Oh yes, it begins, the beginning of the end."

Someone spoke behind him, "Well, that was impressive, and I must say disgusting and a little insane."

Jason spun around to see a group of men in suits. Jason pointed his knife at them.

"Looks like I'm not finished yet," he said as they all pulled out guns and pointed them at Jason pausing him in his tracks.

"Who... who are you?" Jason asked.

"Who am I, huh? A lot of people ask me that, kid. Some say I'm a monster... murderer... Others even call me a businessman; the name's George... George Spire, and I just so happen to be the godfather of the biggest mafia in the state," the man in front said.

"Why are you telling me this?" asked Jason.

"Well, that depends. What's your name, kid?" George responded.

"Jason... I am Jason."

George continued, "Well, Jason, I just saw you kill three men, three men single handed, very impressive, but I did also see something else. I saw you love every moment of it... every hit... every drop of blood... Now some people after

19

seeing that would call you a psycho and call the cops, but I am not one of those people.

"I am businessman, and I don't see a manic. I see an asset... an asset with a high amount of skill, so what I'm saying, Jason, is I would like you to join me and the Spire family mafia and put your skills to good use... better use than slaughtering filthy drunks in the park."

Jason paused as he slowly placed down the knife when George put out his hand.

"What do you say? I'll make it worth your while," Jason shook it.

"Good, this is the start of what I am sure will be a very successful partnership. Here's my number. Call me in 24 hours, and I'll tell you where to go for your first day on the job. Now scoot off. We'll take care of the mess here," George said.

"Why do you want me. Aren't you afraid of me... afraid I could kill you too or rat you out or even steal some money from you?" Jason asked.

"The first yes, but the other two no. I can tell you don't just care about the money. You like the violence," George chuckled.

"I look forward to my first job," Jason smiled and said.

"As do I," George said.

Jason walked off, while the thugs began cleaning up of the bodies.

Jason turned the corner staring at the card and number and spoke to himself, "This... this is good. This will help me commit more chaos than I ever could on my own with the backing of a mafia. I could do so much more... be more...

hahahahahaha. Oh, this is going to be beautiful, just as planned."

Someone yelled from a window, "HEY, SHUT IT DOWN THERE."

"I'm sorry sir. It won't happen again," Jason looked up and said.

"Freak," the man in the window said as he went back inside.

Jason's face crunched in anger.

"You will regret that, sir, in due time, hahahaha," he said.

Jason was being welcomed into a mansion with dozens of guards. He entered and looked around in amazement. George and his two sons were there to welcome him.

"Anthony, Michael, meet Jason the special case I told you about," George said.

Michael stepped forward and shook Jason's hand.

"Dad told us about you. It's a pleasure to meet you. Tell me, do you do karate… judo…?"

"Both can never be too prepared. Now can we?" Jason said.

"I like him," Michael said.

Anthony didn't reach out his hand and instead said to his father, "Are you sure we can trust him. You did pull him out of the street after seeing him murder three men."

"Like we haven't done worse, we will find out if we can trust him. Come, have a drink," George scoffed. They all entered the living room where George poured a whiskey for the four of them.

"No, I'm good," Jason said.

"Is it because you're underage? Asking because I think you've done worse," George said.

"No no. It disrupts the mind, makes me loose concentration," Jason said.

"Very well. Now let's cut to the chase. I would love to welcome you into our family, Jason. You have a skill that we find particularly useful, but you see, you have to prove to me, to us, to the family that you can be trusted and will follow orders. Is that clear?" George asked.

"Crystal?" Jason scoffed.

George smiled and stood up. "Good, I will look for a job for you to prove yourself," George said.

"Oh, one last thing," Jason said.

"Yes, what is it?" George said.

"Give me a… juicer," Jason said.

"Very well, if you insist," George said.

Michael stood too.

"Let me help you, dad." They exited the room.

"Are you really going to help me, or are you just trying to get into my liquor cabinet?" George asked.

"Can't I do both?" Michael asked as they just left earshot.

"Alright now, they're gone. Tell me why do you want to join the family, huh? Is it money… power… or are you just a rat?" Anthony instantly said.

"Oh, you close-minded creature," Jason laughed.

"Excuse me," Anthony said.

"Don't you see the bigger picture. I've seen what the family can give me. You can give me an opportunity… an opportunity to achieve the dream I've had since I was a mere child," Jason replied.

"What kind of dream?" Anthony leaned forward and asked.

Jason smiled and leaned forward, too.

"My dream… My dream to burn it all down… (Anthony shot backwards in horror.) Hahahaha… oh, don't look so shocked, Anthony. You never seen a monster before? Given your position, I thought you would have come across many," he replied.

"Well, your right there. I have seen many so-called monsters, but they all end up the same… dead in a ditch," Anthony said.

"Oh, but I… I am more than a normal monster. I am the devil himself," Jason said.

Anthony jumped to his feet in fear, and anger spurted out.

"You're crazy, and we don't work with crazy."

Jason jumped forward and pinned Anthony against the wall.

"Crazy… crazy doesn't begin to describe me. Now sit down and let me show you and your brother and father why I am the monster you need. Are we at an understanding? OK, good," he whispered in his ear. Jason stroked Anthony's cheek who slapped away his hand as they both sat back down.

Michael and George re-entered the room. "I've got the perfect job for you my friend," George said.

Jason sat back starring at Anthony.

"I'm all ears," Jason said.

"Good, there's a store downtown, and you see, the owner hasn't paid his… let's say fee. So we need you to retrieve his fee. Is that alright?" Michael replied.

"Do I have permission to kill?" Jason asked.

"What? Of course not. Why would we?" Anthony said.

George cut off his son.

"Yes, full permission," George said.

Jason smiled.

Anthony said, "Are you kidding me? We'll lose his store if we kill him."

"Don't be ridiculous, Anthony. Someone else will simply take his place," George said.

"Yeah, it's the way of life," Jason agreed.

"So do you accept?" asked George.

Jason smiled, "YES, I ACCEPT."

Jason entered a small store. He looked around, knocking things off shelves before opening a carton of milk and drinking it.

The person behind the counter yelled, "Sir, sir… you have to pay for that."

Jason stopped drinking and licked his lips as he approached the counter slamming down the milk.

"How much?" Jason enquired.

"$2.50," the cashier said.

Jason pulled out some money to pay.

"Listen here (looked at nametag), Greg; isn't it? I need to see your boss. We have business to discuss… just some simple business…" he said.

"Sorry, sir. But the boss isn't seeing anyone right now. I could schedule you an appointment," Greg replied with a hint of fear in his voice.

"No, it's fine. I understand. I understand. I'll just go. OK?" Jason nodded his head. Jason started leaving but then tossed the milk at the cashier and grabbed him, slamming him onto the counter.

"Please… please… just take the money. Don't hurt me," Greg screamed.

Jason smiled and replied, "Oh no, I'm not a petty thief, Greg. Hmmm… no, I'm a vessel. A normal thief would've

24

ran off with the money, but I don't want the money. I want to send a message. Now what's about to happen? I'm not going to lie to you, Greg. It will hurt.

"It will be excruciatingly painful, and I will enjoy it, Greg. I will savour every moment of it," Jason threw Greg over the counter into a wall, then grabbed his throat and squeezed staring into Greg's eyes until snap. Jason dropped Greg's body as it smacked into the floor.

"Silly me, I thought you'd have a stronger neck. I guess I'll have to take more out on your boss. What a shame!" Jason said.

Jason then walked into the back of the shop straightening his hair and knocked on a door when the owner opened it instantly slamming it shut in panic, but Jason kicked down the door. The owner punched Jason in the face, but Jason didn't even move from the punch, and Jason punched the owner again and again, beating him to a pulp before pulling out a knife, grabbing the owner's arm and cutting off one of his fingers. The owner screamed in agony. Jason grabbed the owner by the hair and cut off an ear, then threw the owner into a chair yelling, "SIT DOWN, or you'll lose a hell of a lot more."

The owner stayed seated holding his head to stop the blood pouring out. Jason said "Good. Now let's put that little scuffle behind us and have a nice chat."

Jason grabbed a chair and slid in closely towards the owner and said, "Why do you look so sad. It's only one ear and one finger. I've taken a lot worse and a lot more. This one time, when I was 17 and was walking down the street, just minding my own business, someone pulled a knife on me. Yeah, I know can't you believe it.

"He kept jittering demanding my wallet. I just couldn't help but laugh. He was so nervous, despite being the one holding the knife. So I kicked the knife out of his hand and smashed his head into a wall. His nose shattered. You could see the bone sticking out in multiple pieces. It was art, but I then took him somewhere nice and private, where I had a nice chat with him, very similar to this one.

"We're having right now, and I got a little carried away. You wouldn't want to know what I did. Ah, screw, you know. How it feels? So what I did is, every time he breathed, I removed a piece of him, starting with his toes and fingers and finishing with his face."

"Oh god," the owner moaned in pure fear.

"HEY, I'm not finished yet. That's so rude of you. If you do that again, we can play the same game." Jason smacked him across the face saying, "Now where was I? Oh, yeah, so I started with the nails. I ripped each and every one out. Some took more than one go as they. Huh… well, they sort off broke apart.

"Then I went for the fingers then the toes and then the ears. Then my favourite, you see, he just wouldn't stop screaming. It got very annoying, so next time this guy stuck out his tongue when he screamed, I grabbed it with my hand, but I didn't simply cut it off. You see, he had enraged me with his nonstop howling. So I pulled and pulled, pulled and pulled until I tore it out. It was very beautiful, and he stopped screaming."

"What do you want? Money? It's all over there… just take it… O OK? I won't tell nobody, I swear," the owner groaned.

"What's your name?" Jason smiled and chuckled.

The owner didn't speak, and after a slight pause of silence, Jason jumped forward smashing his face into his and shouted, "WHAT'S YOUR GOD DAMN NAME?"

"Joseph, I… it's Joseph," the owner cried.

Jason sat back down and said, "Alright. Now listen here, Joe, can I call you Joe?"

Joseph nodded in fear.

"Good, so, Joe, I personally don't really care about the money. That's what the boss wants. He sent me here to collect it, but I really only want one thing, Joe, and do you know what that is? For you to bleed… so I'm gonna put you through more misery than you can imagine. Then I'm gonna take that money to the boss, so, Joe, you better start to brace yourself because this is going to be long and unbearably painful."

Joe screamed. Jason grabbed him and tied him to the chair. Jason then shoved his knife into Joe's finger and ripped out his fingernail. Joe screamed in agony. Jason said, "Hmmm… don't worry, Joe, your mediocre life will soon be over." Jason ripped out another one.

Jason was waiting in the mansion's living room wiping his knife from blood. George, Michael and Anthony all entered.

"There he is. Well, how did it go?" George asked. Jason tossed the bag of money towards him. Michael caught it and dumped it onto the table.

"Well, I'll be damned, and how cooperative was good old Joseph?" George asked.

Jason smiled, "Oh, he was very cooperative, but I wouldn't imagine you'll be seeing him again. He wanted to go for a little swim."

"We've been dealing with Joseph for years. There was no need to kill him," Anthony said.

"Anthony, quiet down. He did his job, just like we asked," George shouted over Anthony.

"Yeah, man, relax. We got the money. All's good," Michael said and annoyed.

"What about the body? The cops… they'll…" Anthony said looking shocked.

"Don't worry about that. Good old Joe and his cashier are at the bottom of the sea. You really think I'd just leave them there. This isn't my first go around, and I've been doing this since I was 12 years old," Jason interrupted.

Anthony and Jason stared each other down.

"That's enough. Now, Jason, I think we can all agree that you have more than proven yourself, so I ask you… do you swear loyalty to the family and swear to serve its best interests till death?" George yelled.

Jason smiled staring at Anthony and said, "I solemnly swear. I pledge myself to the family."

George smiled.

"Excellent, I can't wait to see the great things we will do together. Now, if you would, please leave us," Jason stood and stared at Anthony as he exited.

"You can't be serious. That man is a maniac. He's unpredictable. He can't be trusted. He can't be controlled," Anthony shouted.

"Relax man," Michael replied. "A manic can be useful."

"Your brother's right, Anthony. Jason is an asset, a man with no regret… no filter… no remorse… who can be more useful and more deadly than 10 sane soldiers," George added.

"But," Anthony said.

George cut him off saying, "No, that's enough. I will hear no more of this. Jason is one of us. He will be loyal, or he will see our true power. Do you understand, son?"

Anthony paused before forcibly saying, "OK, you're the boss, dad."

Michael replied, "Good now. Shall we celebrate? I'll get the booze."

Jason was sitting at a bar drinking a glass of milk, scribbling onto the bar.

"Milk really?" asked the woman who was sitting next to him.

"What can I say? I've grown a taste to it," Jason laughed.

"The name's Sarah, and you are?" the woman asked.

Jason smiled and turned to her saying, "Jason... I'm Jason."

"Well, Jason, can I buy you a drink, a real drink?" Sarah asked.

"You can buy me another milk," Jason said.

"Very well... So tell me about yourself, Jason," Sarah said.

Jason downed his milk and said, "Where to begin."

Jason awoke and saw Sarah sitting in a chair across the room.

"Look, who's finally awake? How you are feeling?" she asked.

Jason sat up and rubbed his face, "I feel great."

"Yeah, me too," Sarah laughed. "My number's on the side. You should call me, and we could hang out some more."

Jason stood and walked toward her. She watched this through her mirror while she was doing her hair.

"Oh, I never caught your last na…" Jason grabbed the necklace around her neck and started strangling her.

She struggled but stood no chance.

Jason said, "Sh… sh… sh… it's OK, Sarah. It's not you. It's me. I… I think we should see other people, well, at least I will."

Sarah's body dropped and became lifeless. Jason threw her onto the bed and sat at her desk and started writing a note, "So the tale begins. I wonder who the batman to my joker will be… the knight in shining armour to my monster… hahahhahahahahaha…"

He then ignited a piece of paper and set off the smoke detector before leaving.

The police were in Sarah's room. The area had now become a crime scene. Two detectives walked in: one older around 40 and wise and the other young around 22 and new to the job. The older one (Detective Harvey) walked in.

"Jesus, 18 years on the job, and this never gets less disgusting," Harvey said.

The younger one (Detective James) said, "You can say that again."

"Oh, just you wait, rook. There are some monsters out there," Harvey said.

James asked the forensic, "What've we got?"

"Well, detectives, this is Sarah Kelly. She's 21 years old and was working at a local café in the area. The time of death is around 8:30 am," the forensic replied.

"8:30? That was only two hours ago. How was the body discovered so quickly?" James asked.

"Her smoke detector went off, and when the fire brigade arrived, they discovered the body," the forensic answered.

Harvey looked around. "It doesn't look like there was a fire in here to me," he said.

"Well, technically, there wasn't. (He picked up a evidence bag with burnt paper inside.) It appears that this piece of paper was the source of the fire," the forensic said.

"What time did the alarm go off?" James asked.

The forensic looked through his notes and answered, "8:47."

"That's odd because I'm not sure a dead woman is starting a fire," James said.

"Yeah, I would have to agree with you there," Harvey said.

"The alarm going off a few minutes after she was killed is also very coincidental," James said.

"Which means it was triggered by the killer," Harvey exclaimed.

"So the killer wanted us to discover the body. Did they leave anything behind... maybe a calling card... a note?" James asked.

"Yes, they left this... a note," the forensic said.

Harvey took the note and said, "Well, this is a tad disturbing."

"What does it say?" James asked.

Harvey read it to James, "Hello Officer, whoever is reading this, you have been chosen by fate to be my hunter... to be the one who dedicates his life to stop me... and I cannot wait for our cat and mouse chase to begin, but first, here are some coordinates for a special gift I made just for you. I hope you like it, from your new obsession."

"That doesn't sound very inviting to me," James said.

Harvey sighed.

"Congratulations, man, your first day on the job, and your first case is a psychopath. Welcome to the force, rook. It doesn't get any easier."

"What do you think he means by a gift?" James asked.

"Let's follow the coordinates and find out, but I doubt it's a new car. I'll call it in; get somebody there faster," Harvey said. They left the scene. "Let's just hope this psychopath isn't also a serial killer."

They both stood at the docks looking down.

"Well, I spoke to soon," Harvey said.

Two bodies lay side by side freshly pulled from the water: Greg and Joe.

"I thought the last one was disgusting," Harvey said.

James examined Joe's hand saying, "Well, Harvey, it appears our killer is crazier than we thought."

"What do you mean?" Harvey asked.

James lifted up Joe's arm revealing missing fingers and fingers nails.

"Oh god," Harvey replied. Now that's a new one. Hey, Steve, what's the time of death?"

"By what we can tell, these victims died roughly around 2:00 yesterday," Steve replied.

James rose. "Yesterday, so our killer killed these two before Sarah," James stated.

"Well, James, I hope you're ready," Harvey sighed.

"Ready for what?" James asked.

"A killer," Harvey answered. "A killer like this is gonna take years to find. Trust me, I've dealt with people like this before, so I hope you're ready for a lot of paper work."

Jason watched the detectives through a security camera, as he was painting. He said to himself, "So, Detectives Harvey and James, you are the ones destined to face me. Let us see if you can stop the fire… stop death itself."

Hanging the painting, Jason said, "Let the end begin."

Chapter 3

Eight years later, Jason was waking up from sleep in a new house. As soon as he awoke, he started getting ready for work. (Music played). He put on some clothes, brushed his teeth, went to eat breakfast, but then skipped breakfast and drove through the city to a coffee shop. While he was waiting for his coffee, the music was resumed on the TV, and an announcement appeared.

"Breaking news... the serial killer who was called by many as the Reaper has claimed yet another victim. The killer appeared eight years ago and has taken the lives of over 30 known victims. Should we question our police, and why this monster continues to roam the streets, without consequence? How long we can sleep at night without fear of this monster?"

Jason smiled as he turned to another customer.

"Horrible, isn't it?" he said.

"Oh yeah, it's awful. I don't know how someone like that can sleep at night," replied the customer.

"Like a baby," Jason said.

"What?" the woman said.

Jason took his coffee.

"They sleep like a baby," he repeated and walked off as the woman looked confused. Jason entered into his car and drove away.

Jason arrived at a fancy party at George's mansion. He exited his car as a valet took his keys. Jason walked toward the house doing up his top button on his suit as he entered. The lobby was full of fancy decorations and dozens and dozens of fancily dressed people, as Jason was offered a glass of champagne. He took a champagne glass and poured it into a flower vase before filling the glass with milk. Michael walked up to Jason and said, "There is the main man."

"Drunk already, Michael?" Jason said.

"Nah… I'm fine. Ooh, is that whiskey?" Michael exclaimed and walked away.

Jason sipped his milk.

Then George took the stage and spoke.

"Hello all, I would like to thank you for coming to celebrate the largest and most successful year we have ever seen in family history."

Everyone cheered as George continued, "And we can thank one man above all, a man whose ruthlessness and skill has brought us in more money and more success than we could have ever dreamed of, and that man is here today with us, and his name is Jason Mitchells."

Everyone turned to Jason and clapped for him.

George said, "Now let's toast to a great eight years of service and in hope for many more. Cheers to Jason."

Everyone toasted. Suddenly dozens of people collapsed gagging for air. Everyone panicked, but Jason looked around un-panicked and completely calm.

Detective Harvey and James arrived outside the mansion and got out of their car.

Harvey said, "Oh boy, I should not have had that Mexican yesterday."

"Can you be professional for five minutes?" James said.

"When you've been on the force as long as I have, you sort of loose your filter," Harvey laughed.

James asked another detective.

"What happened?"

"Poison. Somebody poisoned the drinks. Fourteen dead… all members of the family," the detective answered.

James asked, "Family?"

Harvey pulled him aside and spoke, "Listen, James. You've been with us for eight years now. We've become great friends, and I'm sorry we haven't told you about them, but the reason is that the family is the largest crime organisation in the city and the state so try and keep your cool hero boy."

"Oh, so they're all criminals. They're part of the mafia," James asked.

"Shhhhh… keep your voice down. Alright now let's get in there and solve the crime. OK?" Harvey said.

"Why haven't I heard of them before?" James asked.

"We don't really like to talk about them because everyone who does usually ends up missing, so please keep your mouth closed unless it's about the case. Alright?" Harvey asked.

"No promises," James said.

They entered the mansion.

"Damn, now here's what they don't tell you in the academy, the criminals live better," Harvey said.

James asked a cop, "Where are the witnesses?"

"They're waiting in the living room," the cop said.

James and Harvey entered the living room where the survivors were waiting including Michael, Anthony, George, and Jason.

"Alright now. Here's what's gonna happen. Everyone is going to leave the room, and we will call you in one by one and ask questions. Is that understood?" James asked.

The witnesses all nodded. Everyone had been interrogated by Harvey and James. Then they got to Jason. Harvey said looking at a list.

"Next is Jason Mitchells."

Jason took a seat looking at James like a fanboy.

Jason said, "You're James Tyler, aren't you? Lead detective for the serial killer ahh? What's he called? Oh yes, the Reaper!"

James looked confused but replied, "Yes, I am and…"

Jason interrupted, "I'm a big fan. How's the case going? Any new clues? Any leads of his next target?"

"Do you mind if we ask the questions here?" Harvey said.

Jason looked annoyed, "Very well, ask away."

"What were you doing at the party. Why were you invited?" James asked.

"I'm a friend of the family. We were celebrating a business boom," Jason replied.

"And do you know anyone who would want to target the family?" James added.

"Oh, please don't play dumb with me, detective. I think you know quite a few people would like to do this to the family," Jason scoffed.

"Hard to argue with you there. Well, Mr Mitchells," James replied.

Jason interrupted and said, "Jason… call me Jason."

"OK, Jason, where were you when the poison took effect?" James asked.

"Same place as everyone else, the middle of the lobby, toasting to a fine year," Jason answered.

"Somebody says they saw you pouring your champagne into a plant before the toast. Why's that?" Harvey asked.

"I don't drink. I emptied it to fill it with milk. I find that much more… refilling," Jason said.

Then George burst in and demanded, "That's enough questions. We're leaving."

"Look sir, this is a police inves—" James was trying to say something.

But George interrupted, "Don't speak to me like that, Officer. You know who I am, so quiet down unless you'd like to lose your job."

James went to speak when his phone rang. He picked it up.

"Look honey, I'm in the middle of something. I'll call you back. Alright?" he said.

Jason smiled at James and asked, "Is that your wife?"

"Fiancée," James replied.

"Congratulations, I wish you a fabulous wedding," Jason responded.

George said, "Come now, Jason, we're leaving; we don't have to indulge in this."

George stormed off.

"Sir… SIR…" James yelled, but Harvey held him back and said, "Don't… let him go."

Jason walked away.

"It was a pleasure to meet you, James. I do hope to see you again. Oh, and good luck with the case. I'm sure it will be invigorating," he said.

Jason climbed into a limo with George, Anthony and Michael. Michael shouted, "Those pigs don't know who they're talking to, questioning me like a commoner, disgraceful…"

"That's not important right now. What's important is who tried to poison us," Anthony added.

"Agreed, we can't let an act like this stand. Otherwise, we come across as weak. We must take action before the police, and we must put our top man on the job. Jason, would you find who did this and make them pay. Send a message," George added.

"But fa…" Anthony burst out.

But George cut him off raising his hand to silence him and said, "Please, Jason, you're the only one I trust with something this important."

Jason smiled. "It would be an honour, and I swear to you whoever did this will suffer beyond imagination," he replied.

"Good, get to it," George said.

James and Harvey were back at the station looking over the evidence as Harvey put down the phone and said, "Alright, so we have three suspects who don't have an alibi and have a long rivalry with the victims: the Satroni family, the Weasley family and the Green family, who all just happen to be crime organisations."

"Yeah, but what evidence points to either of them. We've got nothing connecting them to the crime, only past feuds," James added.

"You're right. We have no evidence… only the poison, which could be any of them. That's it. This is going to be a long night," Harvey said and picked up the phone again.

"Who you calling?" James asked.

"Pizza places. I'm hungry, and I'm not working on an empty stomach," Harvey answered.

"Can I get some?" James sighed. All through the evening, they looked over the board working.

James jumped to his feet waking up Harvey and said, "I've got it. I've actually got it."

"What? How? Wait, have you slept?" Harvey asked.

"No, but look… look," James said.

"What am I looking at?" Harvey asked.

"Well, by the menu of the event, we know there were three drink options: wine, champagne and whiskey," James said.

"Yeah, so…" Harvey asked.

"Look every victim ordered champagne," James said.

"Yeah, but Jason Mitchells also ordered champagne and didn't…" Harvey sighed.

James excitedly jumped forward interrupting Harvey and said, "Yes, that's right, but what did Jason Mitchells tell us when we questioned him. He doesn't drink alcohol. He poured the champagne away. So he didn't drink it."

"Yeah, but even if you are right, that still doesn't help us," Harvey said.

Then James pulled out a folder saying, "Oh yeah… read this. The champagne was provided by company 42 who just so happen to be owned by…"

"The Green family…" Harvey interrupted. "You genius son of a bitch. I could kiss you. Call it in. We're gonna need back up."

They rushed around to get ready and exited the police station. Jason was sitting in a van with several armed guards

40

listening in on the conversation through the cameras they placed earlier.

"Thank you for the assist, James. I owe you one. The Green family farm now… go, go, go… " he said.

Jason and the van pulled up to the Green family farm. When Jason exited the van, two guards approached him yelling, "What do you want? This is private property."

Jason walked toward them and said, "Relax, guys, relax. I'm only here to talk."

"Who are you?" the guard asked.

"You don't know me. Well, I am…" Jason explained. Suddenly, Jason pulled out two handguns and unloaded into the guards. They both drop to the ground. Jason finished and said, "Death… I am death."

Six soldiers climbed from the van. All armed to join Jason.

Jason said, "Kill them all… no survivors."

Jason ran into the farm running through gun fire from both sides, taking cover behind a tractor. A guard turned the corner coming face to face with Jason. Jason whacked the guard across the face, grabbed his arm punching him in the stomach and flipping the guard over his back breaking his arm so the bone pierced the skin.

Another guard turned the corner. Jason kicked the gun from his hand, then spun around doing a spinning kick into his face. Turning back around, Jason ripped the broken bone from the other guard's arm thrusting it into the stomach of the other guard and then into his jugular.

Jason said, "Congratulations, you have been freed."

Jason then ripped the bone back out spraying blood everywhere as he wiped some onto his fingers and licked it

41

saying, "Hmmm… disgusting…" and walked back over to the other guard attempting to crawl away before Jason plunged the bone in the back of his neck again and again and again. Then he let go and looked up at the sky with blood covering his face and said, "Oh… sweet death, my old friend, you are truly beautiful."

Jason rose picking up the guard's assault rifle and firing it toward several other guards killing them all. Suddenly, Jason was shot in the arm by a rifle knocking him over. Jason laughed yelling, "Ohhh… that hurt hahah…"

Jason jumped to his feet and grabbed one of his own men and used him as a human shield as he pushed toward the house. The human shield was shot repeatedly with holes being blown into him. Jason finally reached the house. He threw the now-dead human shield into the glass door shattering it.

A guard jumped out of the shadows and stabbed Jason in the gut. Jason head-butted the guard, then grabbed his head, ripped out a shard of glass from the door and thrusted it into his eye. Jason pushed further into the house and shot two more guards.

When reaching the living room, one guard unloaded at Jason causing Jason to leap behind cover. Jason looked over his cover and saw the guard standing under a metal sharp chandelier. Jason shot the chain dropping it on the guard impaling him.

Jason then exited the house and headed to the barn while gun shots were still being fired in the background. When Jason reached the barn, he creaked open the door saying, "Henry, oh Henry, Henry Green… I know what you did… and death has come for you. You cannot hide from me. I will

burn this whole farm to the ground if that is what it takes…
HENRY…"

Suddenly, Henry (leader of the Green family) tackled Jason into a wall, but Jason kicked him back, then punched him on the face again and again dodging everyone of Henry's swings until Henry collapsed to his knees. After one last punch, Jason dragged Henry to a corner dropping him there and said, "I have to say, Henry, you do have a strong tackle there. Maybe, in another life, you could have been an NFL player."

Henry spat blood on Jason's face and said, "I did what I had to. They killed my son. I'll pay you double if you leave and kill George instead. I'll make you head of the Green family. I can make your dreams come true."

"Wow, what an offer, Henry! I'm impressed," Jason laughed.

(Henry looked confident thinking he had won.)

"No… unfortunately, I must decline."

"What? You're loyal to him… that rat?" Henry asked.

"No, you don't understand, Henry. Others may think he has all the power in the world, but in reality, he has nothing. I don't care about money. I only want chaos," Jason said.

"And, as head of the Green family, you can cause chaos, as much as your heart contents," Henry said.

"True, very true, but I already have something in motion… something beautiful… something the world will remember… something that will bring this city to its knees… It's a shame you won't get to see it," Jason replied.

Henry now scared and said, "So, all you want is death… and destruction."

Jason smiled and nodded.

"Yes, now you're getting it… I want to watch the world burn. You know, I always wondered what death feels like. It kept me up at night as I imagined its sweet release. Hmmmmmmmmmm… but then one waking night, I discovered it… I realised it… I realised that I am death?"

"What? You're crazy. This is war. Join me, and we can win," Henry said.

"So naïve, Henry. The truth is the only winner in war is death, and I… I am death. Goodbye, Henry. I truly do hope this hurts," Jason said.

Jason grabbed Henry dragging him towards a wood chipper. Jason tossed Henry to the floor and turned it on. Henry climbed to his feet, but Jason shot him in both legs saying, "Trying to run? Are we? What a shame! I thought you'd at least die with honour," Jason pushed Henry into the wood chipper. It ground him into pieces. Henry's screams shattered the cool air, and his blood poured and sprayed out. Jason smiled as his face was sprayed in blood.

Jason turned the chipper off and stepped back looking at his artwork. He licked his lips and said, "Now that… that is what I call art."

Three of Jason's men approached. "It's done, boss. They're all dead," they said.

Jason wiped the blood from his face but ended up just smothering more onto it and asked, "And the others?"

"Dead sir. We're all that's left," the guards said.

Jason nodded.

"Good, that'll make this next part easier," Jason picked up his assault rifle and unleashed bullets eviscerating his men killing them, but one is still barely hanging on and managed to squeeze out.

"W… wwwhy…?" Jason poured gasoline on all of them and stated, "Why? Because why not?" Jason shot the gasoline and set them on fire. He watched them burn to a crisp.

James and Harvey, accompanied by a few dozen other cops, all stood in the farm looking at the carnage.

"Dear god, what happen here?" James said.

"Whatever it was, let's be glad it's not here now," Harvey said.

"These people weren't just killed; they were butchered ripped apart like animals," James sighed in disgust.

"Some people truly are not human," Harvey added.

Then a forensic approached them, "Detectives, you need to see this."

James and Harvey followed the forensic.

Harvey said, "I swear to god if I see—"

Harvey and James froze in horror. They stood in front of Henry Green's body, or what was left of it.

"Please tell me that's not who I think it is," Harvey said.

"That depends. Do you think it is Mr Henry Green? Because that's who it is," the forensic replied.

"This wasn't just a hit. This was personal. Whoever killed him wanted him dead for a personal reason," James said.

The forensic handed them a letter and said, "This was taped to the body."

Harvey held his hand to his head, "Please don't tell me it's from him."

James took the letter in dread and read it aloud:

Dear Detective James, how do you like the art show, one of my finest I will say. I knew you would figure out the case… figure out the poison. I can't wait to embark on the next step of our story together… for the fun has only just begun. See you soon, from your humble acquaintance."

"It's him, isn't it? The killer… the psychopath… We've been chasing for the past eight god damn years… god damn… GOD DAMN IT… This isn't just any other serial killer. This guy… this thing is something else," Harvey gulped.

"But how? How did he kill them all, and why? What personal vendetta did he have against the Greens?" James said.

Harvey still losing his mind quipped, "Who the bloody hell knows? He probably only killed them because he knew we were coming. He's a god damn maniac."

"Harvey, you need to calm down," James said.

"Calm down? You want me to calm down…? Aren't you seeing what I'm seeing?"

James tried to speak.

Harvey continued, "'Cause I'm seeing dozens of bodies… all killed by one man, and the same man that has a personal vendetta against you and me."

James said in frustration, "Harvey, you need to calm down. You've dealt with people like this before."

"The hell I have… I may have been on the force for a long ass time, but this… I've never seen anything like this before, Jim, and… and I'm scared alright. I admit it… I'm terrified of this guy… this thing…" Harvey yelled.

James placed his hand on Harvey's shoulders to calm him down. "It's OK, Harv. It's OK. We'll figure this out, Harvey. Alright. Together, we will take him down. I promise you that."

Harvey calming down said, "OK, Jim, I believe you. Now let's get this piece of shit."

Jason entered a hotel room where Michael, George and Anthony were staying, George asked.

"Well, is it done? Are we safe?" Jason smiled and replied.

"Yes, Henry Green is dead... very dead I might add," George smiled.

"I knew you could do it, always the man for the job, 8 years in and not once have you ever flustered, ever failed (George held Jason's shoulders). You Jason Mitchells are truly like a son to me."

Jason replied, "Thank you, George."

Then Anthony added, "Where are the men you took with you?" Jason sighed.

"Unfortunately, they didn't make it. They sacrificed themselves for the family, fought to their last breath... truly loyal... truly heroic. I couldn't have done it without them."

"Then we will remember their sacrifice," George declared.

Anthony gave Jason an unbelieving look when Michael said, "This is great. We have to celebrate. I'll get the wine."

George laughed, "Always with the booze, aren't you, Michael? Well, while you do that, I'll alert the rest of the family of the good news. Would you care join us in celebrating your success, Jason?"

Jason replied, "No no, I have something else to take care of."

Anthony asked very suspiciously, "And what is that exactly? Surely, you could make time. After all, this is 'your' accomplishment we are celebrating," Jason smirked.

"It is very, very, very important business which I unfortunately cannot discuss with you upright now."

"Very well," George said. "We can celebrate more privately another time perhaps."

"Yes, another time. Goodbye for now. I look forward to the house being reopened."

Jason left, and while Michael and George started celebrating, Anthony watched Jason leaving with untrusting eyes.

Chapter 4

Jason was in a warehouse with five men and one woman tied to chairs… all but one wearing a police uniform. They all woke up from being sprayed by a hose by Jason. Jason shouted, "Wakey… wakey…"

They all panic when one officer said, "What…? Where are we? Who are you?" Jason dropped the hose and spoke, "Oh… come on, you know me, Officer Walker… No? Wow… tut tut tut, I'm the killer you've been chasing for the last few years you know. You're all part of the task force, tasked to bring me down. It's all very flattering to be honest, and this very task force is led by two men, Detectives Harvey and James. You are all members, aren't you? Well, except for you darling, you are much, much more important (Jason got really close to her). You are the fiancée of the dear Detective James Tyler."

"What do you want, freak?" one of the cops yelled.

Jason spun around to this cop and slapped him across the face. "Ha… now that's a name I haven't heard in a while. Nowadays, I go by many names: killer… devil… a monster… the boogie man… even the grim reaper… but freak… freak is one I haven't heard since I was a boy, and that has a great story behind it."

Jason grabbed a steel chair and sat down and continued, "Why don't I tell you the story? I must warn you it is very... disturbing. It may just scar you for life. You see, when I was just a boy all the kids were mean to me. They all picked on me."

"I understand why," one of the cops said.

Jason pulled out a gun and shot the cop in the knee and yelled, "NO INTERUPTIONS."

The cop squealed in pain.

Jason continued, "Now like I was saying, all the kids picked on me... every single day of my pitiful pathetic life, but one above all picked on me the most. His name was Marcus. Huh... it's been a while since I thought of him, little Marcus. Anyway, one day, I fought back against him. I decided to stop the pain... the torment, and I bit out his throat and smashed his head in with a rock. You should have been there. It was very spectacular.

"Probably my favourite kill just for the nostalgia, and I didn't panic at all. I was smart. I hid all evidence, and no one suspected me... not the police... not my parents... No one thought poor little Jason could have killed big ugly Marcus... no one... Except, my dear principal. You see he was one of the only people who knew how much Marcus bullied me because he would watch it. He would love watching Marcus and his friends make my life a living hell, but while the few others who knew of it too simply waved me off, thinking no he's too weak or too innocent to do such a horrific act, but he saw through my lies through my deception, so I took care of it.

"I snuck into his office when I knew he wouldn't be there, and I poured some homemade poison into his morning coffee, and when he drunk from it, his throat erupted open as it burnt through his skin. Blood poured from it, as if I had just opened a faucet. I came out of hiding so he saw me. The last thing he saw before he died was me, the embodiment of death all while he was taken by it.

"After that, it was as easy as forging his handwriting into both a suicide note and a confession of killing poor little Marcus, the case closed, and I had begun my journey into chaos and that my friends, that is what happened to the last person who called me a freak. Well, there was one other, but that is a story for another time. Good story... no?"

Amanda (James's fiancée) said while crying, "What are you going to do to us?"

Jason smiled, "Now that is an even better story, one you're all going to be a part of however unfortunately many of you won't get to see how it ends... But I can tell you the beginning, you are all going to be a part of a special little treasure hunt for Detective James and Harvey. Each clue will have a small time limit, and if they fail to get to the next location and solve the puzzle, then someone dies. More specifically, you die. Good idea, huh? Took me months to plan it out and set up the puzzles.

"I would sit there trying to think of the most brutal deaths I could think of, and I won't lie to you. I got very creative. It truly is a shame. None of you will get to experience them all. Now enough story time. Who will be first? (While he does this, many look horrified, but a few hold it together, with most flinching every time he landed on them.) Ip dip doo, the tiger bites your toe, I rip it in two and drink its blood, so it must be you."

Jason was pointing at Officer Murray who began to break down in tears crying out, "No… no… no… no… please… PLEASE… PLEASE… I beg again."

Jason got right into Murray's face who was completely petrified.

"Oh, I'm sorry, Murray. That's not how the game works." Jason grabbed the back of the Murray's chair and dragged it away all while he screamed in pure fear begging for mercy and help, "NO… NO… HELP ME, PLEASE… PLEASE HELP ME… HELP ME…"

Jason lugged him into the back of a car before entering the driver seat yelled back to the others, "Sit tight and don't move. I'll be back soon."

Jason got in and drove while Murray screamed and wiggled around in the boot crying for mercy, but Jason turned up the music as he drove through the night listening to his songs. All the while Murray kicked and screamed for mercy in the back until finally reaching an open field with four horses tied to a post. Jason jumped out of the car and opened the boot saying, "We're here."

Jason dragged Murray towards the middle. He continued to cry. Jason untied him from the chair and tied his arms and legs to one horse each before sitting down in the chair himself and said, "Well, Murray, I'm sure you can guess what's about to happen, and I'm not going to lie to you. It will be excruciatingly painful, and I am going to enjoy it, but you should know your death is for a greater cause… something bigger than the both of us, and I hope, one day, you will see it. Now, goodbye, Murray."

Jason fired his handgun while Murray continued to beg for his life and all four horses began to run in opposite directions pulling his limbs.

Murray screamed in agony as he was stretched. His skin began to tear. His left leg was torn from his body. Then his right arm and then his right leg. The last horse attached continued to drag him across the field while Jason clapped yelling, "Bravo... bravo... Oh, what a show!"

Jason then got out of his seat and walked to where the last horse stopped and looked down at Murray still alive as blood flowed from him. Jason said, "Still alive? I'm impressed. Truly, I am. Thought someone like you would have died after the first one, but the pain isn't over. You see, because, I still see a limb attached."

Murray barely managed to say, "Pl...e...a...se..."

Jason raised an axe and chopped down on Murray's last limb cutting it off. Blood sprayed onto his face. Jason tossed the axe into a bush after finishing, then wiped the blood on his face using a letter that he then placed inside Murray's mouth. Jason said, "Let the hunt begin."

James and Harvey were in the morgue looking at Murray's body. Harvey said, "Oh god, James, we aren't hunting a man anymore. We're hunting something worse. Oh, Jesus, Murray was like a brother to me. We went to the academy together. What am I going to tell his kids... his wife...? This psychopath has gone too far now... taking cops... innocent cops... my brothers and sisters..."

James scrunched his face in anger. "Tell them... tell his family his killer won't get away with this. I will hunt him down until my last breath if that's what it takes. Call the rest of the task force. We need all hands-on deck," James replied.

Harvey pulled out his phone to call them while James looked at Murray's body. Harvey turned to James and spoke, "James."

James answered, "Yes, what is it?"

"Murray's not the only one he took," Harvey added.

James turned and asked, "What are you saying?"

Harvey said, "I'm saying he's not just taken Murray; he's taken the entire god damn task force."

James asked, "How do you know?"

Harvey placed the phone out as a voice said, "HELLO, JIM."

"What have you done? You've taken innocent cops and are torturing them, is that it?" James questioned.

Jason answered, "Yes, yes, that is exactly what I am doing, but don't worry, I'm not going to kill them, or at least not right now. Check the note dear Murray has for you. I will be watching on the edge of my seat."

The phone call ended as Harvey yelled, "He's taken them all, pulled them from their homes, their families."

James paused, "Then we better save them. This letter was in Murray's mouth. Let's open it up. We'll play this freaks game if we have to." James opened the letter and read:

Hello again, Detectives, how do you like the new Murray. I think he's better this way, much less whiney and a lot less screaming, but that's not my point. I want to play a game… a treasure hunt. How does that sound? You have six hours although for you probably just two now when your reading this, to solve the puzzle, which will lead you to another member of your beloved task force and then another and another, but if your late, you won't be able to save them. Now clue number 1 is a riddle. I do love a good riddle. I'm a lover with a ring, yet am not yet wedded what am I.

"I never was good at riddles," Harvey sighed.

James's heart dropped, "Oh god."

Harvey asked, "What? Do you have the answer?"

"It's fiancée. The answer's fiancée," James replied. James pulled out his phone and called Amanda yelling, "Come on, pick up… pick up… pick up…"

A dark voice answered, "Hello again, Jim, back so soon. Are we?"

James yelled out in rage, "Where is she? What've you done? If you hurt her, I'll …"

Jason interrupted, "What you'll hurt me? Kill me? How can you do that when you don't even know who I am?"

"Oh, I may not know who you are, but I know what you are… a monster," James said.

Jason replied, "Yes, yes, I am. You're finally beginning to understand."

Amanda screamed yelling, "Jim, help me."

Jason yelled back, "SHUT THE HELL UP."

"Look, she has no part in this. She's not in the task force. Just let her go," James said.

Jason laughed replying, "Oh, but she is a part of this so very much so."

"Please just… just let her go," James begged.

"Sorry, I can't do that, Jim. You see, when I learnt you had a fiancée, I thought her being a part of our little game… would give you some extra motivation. Oh… and congrats on solving the first puzzle. Now here's the location of the next, but you better hurry, you've only got 17 minutes to get there, before…" Jason replied.

"Just tell me," James yelled.

"The construction site downtown but you…" Jason answered.

James instantly hung up and ran to his car followed by Harvey.

"Where are we going?" Harvey said.

"Downtown construction site," James replied.

They raced off crashing through objects, scraping past cars and nearly hitting pedestrians.

"Slow down, or you're gonna get us killed," Harvey yelled.

"If I slow down, we won't make it," James yelled back.

They continued their chaotic ride until eventually reaching the site. They jumped from the car and hastily searched. Harvey came across a deep hole. He looked down it and saw Officers Walker and Hernandez stuck at the bottom.

"Jim, over here," Harvey yelled.

James sprinted over and saw them.

"Hurry… help us. That manic put us down here," Walker yelled.

"How are we going to get them out?" Harvey asked Jim.

James saw a ladder and sprinted over to it.

Harvey then looked to his right and saw a cement mixer with a clock on the back counting 5… 4… 3… 2… "James, hurry. There's a timer," Harvey yelled.

The cement mixer opened.

"NOOOO…" Harvey yelled as the mixer dumped tons and tons of cement onto Walker and Hernandez burying them alive.

"God damn it," Harvey screamed as Jim got back with the ladder, then dropped to his knees in defeat. "This is my fault. I wasn't fast enough. I brought them into all this. I did this to them."

Harvey turned to Jim and spoke, "Hey, don't say that. This isn't your fault. You didn't put them in that hole. Alright. Get it together. We still have two officers and your lady to find, and we can't do that if we sit here moping around."

James shook it off, "Yeah, you're right. Thank you, Harvey."

"Good, now then there has to be a letter around here somewhere, with the next clue," Harvey added.

They searched for the letter. James found it on the driver's chair of the cement mixer. James called Harvey over as he opened it.

"It's just a phone number," James said.

"Call it."

James called it and heard clapping followed by Jason.

"Good try, good try, indeed, a valiant effort. If I do say so myself, but a teeny bit too slow, better luck next time.

"You're gonna pay for this you sick son of a…" Harvey yelled into the phone.

Jason interrupted, "Would you like to keep threatening me, Detective. Maybe I go after your family next… make them suffer with us. How is little Jasmine these days?"

"How do you…?" Harvey said.

"I know everything. I have been studying you both for the past eight years. Each crime I committed that you tried to

57

solve, I learnt more and more about you. Now where was I? Oh, yeah, I was originally going to give you another riddle, but to be honest your already running behind schedule. So just go to the crematorium and don't be late 'cause this one is going to be fire. Hahahahahahaha…" Jason said.

They hung up the phone.

Chapter 5

Jason at the crematorium surrounded by bodies of workers with two people tied to chairs: one the manager of the facility and the other Officer Martin. The manager was terrified while Martin was holding it together.

"How rude of them," Jason said. Suddenly, Jason turned to them slamming down a handgun onto the table causing the manager to jump in fear.

"Leave him alone," Martin said.

"Well, I have to say, Martin, I'm impressed you're not pissing your pants like the others or like this guy, or at least not yet, but your bravery is a lie because, underneath it, you're just as scared as everyone. Every pathetic miserable person on this planet afraid to evolve. Now let's play a game while we wait. Shall we?

"OK, here's the game… this gun in my hand has one bullet… just one. Now whoever grabs it first when I put it on the table has a choice to make. You can either shoot yourself saving the other, or the real interesting part you can choose to shoot the other person and save yourself. Do you understand?" Jason explained.

The manager nodded his head in fear.

"Don't do it. It's a trick," Martin said.

"A trick? I would never…" Jason replied. Jason spun the gun on the table. The manager grabbed the gun instantly, but Martin did not even try. The manager pointed the gun at Martin shaking in fear.

"I'm sorry, but I'm not ready to die. I have a family," the manager said and pulled the trigger, but only water fired out. The manager looked at the gun in confusion. Jason slammed the manager's head into the table and held it there.

"Well, would you look at that. You're not just brave but smart too, aren't you, Officer Martin? Now you've seen it… seen it with your own eyes… seen the fear of death and how it is enough to change the most innocent of man into a monster… a killer… a coward… just like it has done to our friend here. Death brings out the monster inside of us, and yes, I am a monster, but the truth is deep.

"Deep down, we all want to do the things I've done. The only difference between me and you is I wasn't afraid to do it. I wasn't afraid to embrace the monster, instead of running from it. Now say goodbye to our dear manager, Officer Martin, but don't worry, there is no need to miss him because I'm sure you'll be joining him very, very soon."

Jason plunged a knife into the managers eye cutting it out and then smashing it with the managers head. Then he did it again with his other eye as the manager screamed in agony. Jason twisted his bottom jaw and top jaw in opposite direction tearing his face in half.

"You won't get away with this. Fate will catch up to you eventually," Officer Martin said looking sickened.

Jason got right up in his face.

"Oh, trust me, I know, but how much more damage will I cause until it does," he said and smiled.

James and Harvey walked through the facility walking past several corpses.

"He killed them all, every last one of them," Harvey said.

"But why? What part do they play in this?" James replied.

"They don't. They don't play any part. Someone as deranged as this guy is, they don't care about who dies. I bet that sick bastard enjoyed it," Harvey said.

"What if we're too late? What if… what if Amanda's already dead?" James asked.

Harvey grimaced, "Don't think like that. We won't let that happen. This sick son of a bitch isn't gonna win," James continued until finally reaching the cremation room where they saw the manager's disfigured body. They both gagged.

"Jesus Christ," Harvey said when they hear a voice over the speaker saying.

"Hello again, Detectives." James and Harvey both spun around as Jason continued, "Don't bother looking for me. I'm long gone, but brave Officer Martin isn't in fact. He's right there in that room with you now."

Harvey looked around.

"Where is he?" James yelled.

"Close… he's very close. If you look around, you will see 10 furnaces, and inside one of them is Officer Martin, and I'm sure you know what is going to happen to him if you fail to save him, just like you failed to save the others," Jason answered.

"What do we do? Where are the keys?" Harvey asked.

"You will find the keys inside of my friend sitting at the table. He's been patiently awaiting your arrival," Jason said.

"Oh, please don't tell me that means what I think it does." Harvey said.

"Yep, I think it does," Harvey winced.

"Oh, hell no." James laid the managers corpse on the table and cut off his clothes.

"Oh man, James, are you sure about this?" Harvey asked.

"What choice do we have?" James asked.

James placed the knife on him.

"Ready, Harvey?"

"Hell, no, I'm not ready," Harvey said.

James cut into the manager's stomach and shoved his hands in looking for a key.

"Oh, I think I'm gonna puke," Harvey gagged.

"Hurry up, and get in here," James said.

Harvey reluctantly put his hands in gagging every second and spoke, "Sorry, lord, for what I'm about to do."

They search around.

"I… I can't find anything. Oh wait," Harvey said and pulled out what he thought was a key but turned out to be a metal implant. "I don't think this is a key."

"Then keep searching," Jason said.

Harvey put his hands back in, and after a while, James got angry and shouted, "THERE'S NOTHING IN HERE. Where the hell is the key?"

"Hahahaha… I'm joking. Oh, you are so easy to manipulate. Oh, you should see the look on your faces. The key is in his back pocket," Jason laughed.

"Oh, you sick piece of garbage," Harvey yelled. They pulled their hands out and pulled out the key from his pocket.

"OK, that's one now. Where are the other nine?" Harvey asked.

"No no. You don't understand. There is only one you must pick… just one… get it wrong and the pig gets roasted," Jason laughed.

James dropped to his knees.

"Martin… Martin, where are you? Martin…" he yelled (he rushed to every option and banged on them screaming into them). Come on, give us something… a sign, MARTIN…"

Harvey stopped him and said, "He can't hear you, Jim. We're on our own. Give me the key."

"What? Harvey, no. I…" James tried to say something.

"Jim, give me the key. I won't let you have this weigh down on your shoulders for the rest of your life. You don't deserve that brother. Give me the key," Harvey yelled.

"What about your life?" James replied.

"My life… I've already got so much on my shoulders as it is. What's a little more? Please hand me the key, brother," Harvey said.

James hesitated before handing Harvey the key.

"Are you sure?"

"No, but when am I ever?" Harvey asked.

"Ah, how wholesome, NOW PICK ONE," Jason said.

Harvey turned to look at all the options. He walked toward one praying while he did it. Then he turned the key and opened it revealing nothing. Harvey and James looked broken and defeated as Jason spoke, "Too bad… I actually had a little faith in you, but unfortunately, for you and him, it's time to say goodbye to Officer Martin."

A TV in the corner switched on revealing Martin. The furnace activated. He wriggled around in pain as the flames grew larger and larger. Harvey and James began shoving the key in every furnace, each one revealing nothing. All while, Jason laughed.

The flames began to fully engulf Martin. Finally, on the sixth attempt, they pulled open the right one and pulled Martin out. Martin was screaming as his body was covered in burns, and the fire still covered him. Harvey grabbed a fire extinguisher and sprayed Martin putting out the fire. James held Martin and yelled, "Damn it... Harvey, call an ambulance. Listen, Martin, it's me James. You're going to be OK. I'm here for you."

"J... James... I... I... I can't see. It burns," Martin replied.

"Just hold on... hold on, Martin," James said.

"P... prommmmise me... Promise you'll s... ss ... ssstop him..." Martin asked.

"I promise... I promise, Martin... Martin... MARTIN..." James shouted.

"Is he?" Harvey asked.

"He's gone," James said.

"Oh god... you... YOU PSYCHOPATH... ARE YOU ENJOYNG THIS, HUH? ARE YOU?" Harvey asked.

Jason's voice returned saying, "Yes, detective, yes, I am enjoying it, every moment of it."

"Why? What did we or any of these people ever do to you? WHAT DID WE DO TO YOU?" Harvey yelled.

"What did they do to me, detective? Nothing. They did nothing to me," Jason replied.

"Then why? Why are you doing this?" Harvey asked.

"Because... because I want to... I want to watch you suffer with me. Now, if you will turn to the TV, Officer Brandon has a message for you."

They turned to the TV where they saw the last officer, Officer Brandon. He was strapped to a chair an electric chair with a sign around his neck.

Jason answered, "Now, unfortunately, Officer Brandon will not be saved today because I had an extra hostage than planned. So, instead, your last victim is the lovely Amanda. This is your last chance. Detectives… good luck," Jason said.

"Manic," Harvey said.

James read the sign out around Officer Brandon's neck, "You will find me and your love in the place where I was born again."

"What do you thi…?" Harvey asked. Suddenly, the electric chair was activated, and Officer Brandon was electrocuted to death. They both looked horrified.

"So many… so many good people have died today… died because of this… this lunatic. I won't lose her too. I can't lose her too," James said.

"Then we won't," Harvey said. Then, suddenly, the TV switched on revealing the words look inside the box.

"Box… what box?" Harvey said.

James pointed at a cardboard box in the corner, and he rushed over to it and ripped it open. Hundreds of photos fell out.

"What are these? Photos of random people. How are these going to help?" Harvey asked.

James lifted a photo of Henry Green and spoke, "Not random. These are all his victims."

Harvey dropped to his knees. "No no. This can't be. There're so many. There has been hundreds. How many lives has this sick son of bitch ruined?" Harvey said.

"I don't understand. How are these supposed to help?" James asked. James looked through them. He brushed past one, a child.

"Wait, that one, the kid?" Harvey asked.

James picked up the photo.

And Harvey added, "He's not one of his victims."

"Well, we didn't think over half of these were so," James said.

Harvey cut him off.

"No, I know this kid wasn't one of his victims. I was on that case. His name was Marcus. We investigated, but nothing up turned. But then the principal of the school committed suicide and confessed in a letter to the murder."

"But what if he wasn't the killer? What if he was framed?" James said.

Harvey showed fear and shock in his face. "Oh god, before the principal died, he said to me… he said to me that he thought it might have been another student."

James found another picture with a school logo in the background and spoke, "Is this that principal by any chance?"

"Yes, I know who he is. I know who the killer is," Harvey replied gulping.

"Who?" James asked in desperation.

"His name… his name was Jason… Jason Mitchells," Harvey answered.

James looked shockingly, "That's the same guy who works for the Spire family."

"That son of a bitch. He's been in front of our faces the entire time, watching us run around in circles," Harvey added.

"But what does he mean by the place he was born again," James asked.

Harvey jumped to his feet, "His parents' house… it's right by the woods where the body was found… where he killed Marcus… his first victim."

They both said at the same time, "Where he was born again…"

"Let's go now… NOW…" James shouted.

They rushed out leaving the photos behind.

Chapter 6

Jason was sitting in his childhood bedroom looking at all his trophies and said, "It's been a while." He reached under his bed and pulled out the rock he used to kill Marcus and his blooded shirt and said, "It feels like so long ago now, so long since you left me, Marcus. If only you could see what I've become, just like I told you all those years ago, I wish I could kill you again. But the past is the past. I have become something greater than either of us imagined. This is goodbye forever, Marcus."

Jason walked down his stairs where his dad and mum were tied to chairs both bleeding from head injuries and gagged. Amanda was also tied to a chair. Jason ungagged his dad and said, "Hello, dad, how are you? Been eating well... getting some exercise in, I trust."

"J... Jason, what are you doing, my son?" Richard asked confused.

"I'm doing what I've always wanted to do, dad. Be different... be something more... escape the NORMAL LIFE OF REPITION EVERY OTHER PERSON LIVES ON THIS GOD FORESAKEN ROCK... I have broken through the boundaries of society. I have broken the natural world order, and to think, all it took was a couple meaningless people to die... to suffer..." Jason replied.

"What have you done, son? What have you become?" Richard asked.

"I have become something more, dad. Something bigger… something greater… something different. I have become a monster, one so scary… so unmatched that even those monsters, the ones from those stories you used to read to me as a kid, even they hide from me now. They tremble at the thought of me," Jason laughed.

"What about the man, the son I once knew?" Richard asked.

"The man in me died, a long, long time ago, and I am what emerged from his demise," Jason said.

"I loved you, son. You were my everything. I LOVED YOU. WE LOVED YOU."

Richard was crying.

Jason smiled, "I know you did (he got really close to his dad), but the truth is… I never loved you," Jason started smashing his father's head with the sharp rock he used to kill Marcus. He hit him again and again and again until his father was more than dead.

Jason laughed falling to the ground in uncontrollable laughter and began punching the ground before rising to his feet and shooting his mother in the head. He suddenly stopped laughing and said, "Huh… it's almost as if I regret doing that, but I did it. Hahaha… I did it. I have now truly become something more. I have won."

He turned to Amanda who was sitting petrified.

"Don't worry now. I'm sure Detective James will save you. I am sure it won't be long until he comes running through that door to save you like the knight in shining armour. He thinks he is, so I guess that makes you the princess and me what… the dragon… (he rubbed Amanda's face), but until then… until he arrives to save you… you will suffer."

Jason picked up a hammer and began to smash Amanda's hand… whacking it again and again… crushing the bones… He heard a car pulling up.

"I'll be damned. They solved it faster than I thought. I'm sorry our time had to be cut short. This is goodbye Amanda, but I'm sure we'll meet again," he said.

Jason ran out the back but not before turning on the gas and throwing a lighter into the corner. James and Harvey burst in.

"AMANDA," James said.

And they rushed to Amanda. They started untying her and ungagging her as she groaned in pain.

James said, "Oh god, Amanda. What did he do to you? It's OK. I'm here. We're going to get you safe and to a hospital. OK?"

Harvey searched the kitchen and saw the flame and heard the gas. He ran out yelling, "Get down."

A massive explosion happened destroying half the house and setting the rest on fire. James carried Amanda out as Harvey followed. They loaded her into the car and drove for a hospital.

Jason walked through the woods. When he saw the explosion, he clapped saying, "Goodbye, this is the day you have truly died forever. I have severed almost everything connected to me except for this." He pulled out the sharp rock covered in his father's blood and said, "We have done some great things together, haven't we? I know I'm gonna miss you, too, but this is goodbye." He threw the rock away and said, "Goodbye, Jason Mitchells."

Jason walked away. He had flashes of that day… the day he killed Marcus as he travelled past the same locations until he reaches it… his stick house from when he was a kid. He smiled and said, "Finally, my true home."

Jason approached it, and when he got inside, there were two small children inside: a boy and a girl. Jason was surprised and asked, "Well, hello. Who might you two be? My name is… well, it was Jason. I guess you can call me that, but the truth is I no longer have a name."

A woman's voice was heard in the background.

"Jacob, Isabelle, come on… come out of hiding… uh… where have you two gone?" she yelled.

Jason smiled and spoke, "You two hold on. I'll be right back," he exited.

"Oh, hello, you wouldn't happen to have seen two young children. I've been looking for like 10 minutes and… OH MY GOD, NO PLEASE WAIT," the woman said.

Bang, a gunshot, and the sound of a body dropping.

Jason entered the house again, "Sorry for that inconvenience. I take it your Jacob and Isabelle, what wonderful names… Well, it was nice to meet you, but I must get going."

He raised the gun but then saw a new drawing, an exact copy of his drawing of Marcus, and in pure joy, he stopped himself and said, "Wow, did you do this? You both have a beautiful mind."

Jason paused trying to make a choice as he placed down the gun and instead reached out a hand saying, "Come on, let me take you to your new home. I'm sure you're going to love it."

Chapter 7

4 Years Later

Jason was back at his house feeding his two kids some breakfast. He looked at the TV with a news reporter reading, "The killer known as the Reaper after 12 years is still at large. Police lead suspect Jason Mitchells is believed to be the killer according to lead Detectives James and Harvey, but not enough evidence links Mr Mitchells to the killings, leading many to believe his innocence."

"Isn't that you, daddy?" Jacob asked.

"It sure is… it sure is…" Jason laughed saying before sipping his milk.

Later that day, Jason was inside the Spire mansion having a toast with George.

"Can't believe how long it's been since I found you in that park. It feels like only yesterday. And look at what you have accomplished in the years since, cementing your legacy within our family… your family…" George said.

"I too have enjoyed our time together. I too relish in what we have achieved… 12 years well spent," Jason smirked answering.

"So, Jason, tell me, what moment has been your favourite? The highlight of your career with us…" George asked.

Jason stopped thinking, "There are so many to choose from... but one which stands out to me, the assault on the Green family farm... that was a good day."

"That it was... a day of sacrifice and victory... when we vanquished our enemy, but lost some good men in the process," George said.

"That we did... that we did..." Jason agreed.

"However, my favourite moment from your time with us... it holds a very special place in my heart," George said.

"And what would that be, my friend?" Jason asked.

George smiled and spoke, "The day you introduced me to little Jacob and Izzy, seeing you so complete... as if you had changed... Become someone new..."

"Not someone, but something," Jason smiled.

Georges chuckled and asked, "Oh, how are the kids, Jacob and little Izzy? It's been a few months since I saw them. How have they been?"

"They both are doing great. Both want to learn some martial arts," Jason answered.

"Ah... learning from the master himself..." George said.

"Yes, and making excellent progress as well," Jason said.

"Then they have a bright future. Here's to them, cheers," George laughed.

Jason took a sip of his milk.

"Here I have a question," George said.

"Hit me," Jason said.

"Why do you think Anthony distrusts you so much, even these days, even after 12 years of loyal hardworking service from you, and yet he still despises you?" George enquired.

"It's in his nature. It doesn't matter if I was just a waiter for you. He would never trust me, unlike Michael," Jason said.

73

"Oh, don't get me started on Michael. Do you know he spent $300,000 in a week... A WEEK... Can you believe that?" George sighed.

"Knowing Michael, yes, I can very easily believe it. What did he spend it on?" Jason asked.

"Who knows, probably booze, or drugs maybe even a couple strippers? You know, Michael still hasn't learnt to grow up. Let's just sit and hope Jacob doesn't end up like him or god forbid Izzy," George replied.

"Oh, they wouldn't dare," Jason said.

George and Jason laughed although it was obvious that Jason was faking.

Jason asked, "So what's the job?"

"You know that's what I love about you. Your mind is always on the job... never distracted. If only you were one of my sons, I would be able to die in peace knowing everything I spent my life building would be safe, but knowing my sons, half of it will fall within a year of my death," George answered.

"Oh, don't be silly, George. It'll be a lot faster than that," Jason said.

George laughed again. George drank again and spoke, "The job is a tricky one, a high value target, you see as you know. I have Mayor Jenkins in my pocket. He's my little puppet, but he doesn't seem to be winning enough votes to stay in his position, and I've tried paying people off. I've even paid for advertisements for his campaign, but none of it has worked, and before you ask, his competition has nothing, nothing to black mail him with, and he won't accept bribes. He is actually believe or not a good man; it's a shame that he plots against us; maybe he could clean this city up, but alas, I need you to please take care of him for me."

"Any restrictions?" Jason asked.

"No, do whatever is needed, and whatever it is, make sure it's big. I don't want anyone trying to take over from him. You got it?" George said.

Jason downed his milk, "Don't worry. After I'm done with him, no one will ever wish to run for mayor again."

"That's my man. Here's his address," George said.

Jason took the address and stood up. George said, "Oh, you're going now? I thought you were resting."

"I never rest boss… never…" Jason said and walked away.

As Jason left, George smiled and said to himself, "What dedication!" He took a sip of his drink.

Larry DeTroy, the competitor for the mayor, was sitting in a car. The driver said, "Here we are, sir."

"Thank you, Ken. Here for your troubles," Larry said and handed him some money.

"Thank you, sir. You sure you don't want me to drop you closer?" Ken asked.

"No, I'll be fine. A little rain never hurt anyone, and besides, if we even touch my wife's roses, you don't want to know what she'll do," Larry replied.

"Well, OK then, good night, Mr DeTroy," Ken responded.

"Please call, Larry," Larry DeTroy responded.

Larry exited the car as he ran up his drive way and to his house. He entered into it and walked to his living room removing his coat in the dark yelling, "Joseph, Andrew, you still up? No? Honey what about you? No? Alright then."

He walked into the kitchen and started making himself a sandwich. Suddenly, he saw a figure moving around him. He asked, "Honey, is that you? Oh, you're never going to believe what happened at work today? You know five different people tried to bribe me today… five… no wonder this city's in the state that it is."

He switched on the light and saw his wife Mary and two kids, Andrew and Joseph, all sitting in chairs with their throats slit. Larry froze and yelled, "Oh god… oh god… no…" He turned around to run for help but met face to face with Jason.

"Boo."

Larry walked backwards and fell over dropping his sandwich on the floor. He was panting in fear. Jason took a bite of his sandwich. Larry rose to his feet grabbing a lamp yelling, "You killed them… YOU KILLED THEM… you son of a bitch."

"Yes, and what are you going to do?" Jason said.

"I'LL KILL YOU," Larry screamed.

Jason opened his arms and spoke, "Go on… take your best shot."

Larry yelled and smashed the lamp across Jason's face.

Jason took the hit, "Is that all?"

Larry swung again, but this time, Jason grabbed the lamp and headbutted Larry on the face. Larry fell backwards into a table. Jason grabbed Larry and spoke, "Shh… the more you struggle, the worse I'll make it hurt."

Jason headbutted Larry again knocking him out. Larry came too tied to a chair and struggled to break free attempting to wiggle out.

"There is no use. Even if you were to break free, what would you do?" Jason asked from the darkness. (Jason slowly stepped out from the darkness). Run, hide, or maybe… just maybe you would fight?"

"I'm not afraid of men like you. You're everything I stand against, the people who corrupt this city, this world, and for what money… POWER?" Larry said.

"WRONG… WRONG… WRONG…" Jason shouted.

"Then why? I know you're working with George Spire. I know he hired you to kill me," Larry said with a stern unafraid face.

"Yes, that is correct," Jason said.

"Then you're in it for money then," Larry said.

"You may have a pure heart. You may have no fear, but your mind is still closed… still unable to see the bigger picture," Jason shook his head.

"Then what is the bigger picture? Go on… enlighten me," Larry frowned.

"I like you, Larry. You're not like most. Most people in your situation would be begging… begging for mercy from me… from god… and praying for help. Even those not religious break and BEG FOR HELP. But none ever comes," Jason smiled.

"Oh, I see now… you're afraid," Larry said.

Jason looked shocked, "Excuse me."

Larry continued, "You're avoiding answering my question. The truth is you don't know why you do this, your hiding, running from the truth."

"I AM NOT AFRAID OF ANYTHING… YOU HEAR ME? NOTHING…" Jason snapped screaming and spitting everywhere.

Larry leaned forward still unafraid, "Then answer the question. Why?"

"You don't deserve the full answer, but I will enlighten you to the short one," Jason said.

"Fine, well, go on. Then tell me," Larry responded.

"Suffering," Jason replied.

"What do you mean by suffering?" Larry asked.

"That's why I do what I do, so you, this city, this state, THIS COUNTRY, THIS WHOLE WORLD CAN SUFFER… suffer with me… feel the pain. I do every waking moment of my life, and don't try and deny it. I know even men like you still live in pain," Jason replied.

"No, you're just a broken pathetic excuse for a man," Larry said.

"See, now who's lying. You're going to sit there and tell me… tell me that you don't feel the pain… the pain of repeating the same day, again and again. You just won't admit it, but I did. I set myself free," Jason said with a deranged look. Jason looked victorious thinking he had broken Larry.

Larry looked more unafraid than before.

"You're wrong." Jason looked shocked as Larry continued. "You're just making excuses, trying to cope with the monstrous things you've done, underneath your skin. You're the same as us all… blood and bone. You are not special. You have not broken free from society. You have merely CRUMBLED BENEATH IT."

Jason lost it punching Larry in the face.

"Did that feel good?" Larry said.

"Yes, yes, it did, and I believe I'll do it again," Jason said and punched Larry in the face again and again and again, but Larry still isn't scared.

"You're even more pathetic than your boss," Jason grabbed Larry's throat.

"Don't belittle me to that… THAT PIG. He is nothing you… Hear me… he is nothing. NOTHING COMPARED TO ME. I AM EVERYTHING. I AM THE ANSWER, ME, NOT HIM… NOT YOU… NOT ANYONE ELSE… ON THIS STUPID WORTHLESS PLANET… ME AND ONLY ME!"

"You keep telling yourself that," Larry said.

Jason's face twitched uncontrollable and walked towards the door and spoke, "You'll see. I'll show you. I will show you all."

Jason opened the door as several rabid dogs ran in and sprinted towards Larry. They started ripping him apart. Jason watched as Larry yelled with his final breath, "You… are… nothing…"

Jason looked enraged and slammed the door closed leaving Larry to die.

Chapter 8

James and Harvey were standing in front of Larry whose legs were nearly completely eaten.

Harvey wiped his brow.

"Jesus, they just keep getting worse. Do you think it's him?"

"Of course, it is. Who else is crazy enough to do this?" James answered.

"How many more have to die before we stop him," Harvey said.

"I don't know, Harv. I don't know. I sure wish I did."

A forensic handed them a letter marked, "Hello again!"

James said, "Well, I think this answered your question. It's definitely him." "Let's see what this sick bastard has to say this time," Harvey said.

James tore it open and read away:

Hello, my dear friends, it's been a while since we met like this, not since that night, you remember the night you failed to save your fellow officers, but anyway, you may be thinking.

I haven't killed since then, but you'd be very, very mistaken. In fact, I've probably killed more in the last few months than ever before. Now I come to you as a warning... a warning that hell is coming... it is coming, my friends, and you won't be able to stop it. It will consume ALL.

"What in god's name does that mean? Hell is coming?" Harvey asked.

"I don't know, but coming from him, it can't be good," "James answered.

"Or maybe he's decided to become religious wash away. His sins turned over a new leaf," Harvey said.

"Well, if he has turned religious, I don't think he's on the good side," James said.

They paused.

Harvey asked, "Hey, how's Amanda?"

"What? Oh, she's fine."

"You sure? Because, last time, I spoke to her she was complaining that a certain someone brought the wrong cereal," Harvey said.

"It's just hormones. That's all," James said.

"Let's hope your second one is less annoying than your first. Last time I came round, he wouldn't stop screaming," Harvey said.

"Well, if they aren't, I'm gonna be sleeping in the shed," James laughed.

Harvey chuckled.

They climb into their car, and James pulled out several fries from between his seat and looked at Harvey.

"Really? What have I told you about eating in the car?"

"It's called a stake out for a reason," Harvey said.

James shook his head. Suddenly, a gunshot was fired through the window flying right between the two of them.

"Oh, shit," Harvey said.

They ducked down, and Harvey yelled out, "You've got to be kidding me, not five minutes of peace in this city."

"Can't catch a break, can we?" James added.

"You can say that again," Harvey replied.

Another shot was fired at the car.

Harvey looked at James, "What's the plan?"

"Just follow my lead," James said.

"Follow your what?" Harvey asked.

James exited the car and rolled into cover.

Another shot barely missed him. "Come on, follow me," James yelled.

"Yeah no, I think I'm good," Harvey replied, looking concerned.

James poked his head up and saw where the gun shots were coming from. A sniper across the street. Another shot was fired and made a small cut across James's face. He ducked back down.

"James, Jesus. You OK?" Harvey asked.

James wiped the blood from his face, "Yeah, I'm good. Just a scratch."

"Did you see where the shots are coming fr—" Harvey asked.

Another shot was fired at the car causing Harvey to flinch yelling, "Holy shit."

"The shots are coming from across the street… over there on that roof," James said.

Another officer ran out into the open, "Detective James, I heard gunshots."

"Get down," Harvey and James both yelled.

A shot was fired into the officer's shoulder. James sprinted out of cover and dragged the officer behind cover.

More shots collided with the ground around him. The cop groaned in pain.

"Harvey, toss me your tie," James yelled.

"What do you need…?" Harvey asked.

"Just give it to me," James interrupted yelling. Harvey took off his tie and threw it to James caught it and held it against the cop's wound. He said, "Hold this tight. Alright?"

The cop nodded.

"You owe me a new tie," Harvey said.

James shook his head.

"Focus, Harvey. OK, here's the plan. You're going to distract him while I sneak over and subdue him from behind. Got it?" James went to get up.

"Woah… woah… hold your horses there," Harvey said.

"What?" James said.

"Why do I have to be the bait? Why can't you do it?" Harvey asked.

"Because the shooter will see you as an easier target," James sighed.

"Is that a fat joke?" Harvey asked.

"Yep," James replied. and ran out of cover.

Harvey went to do the same and said to himself, "Next time, you ask for anything, I swear to god."

Harvey ran out of cover and blindly fired towards the building yelling, "Come get me, you sons of bitches."

Then a gunshot landed right in front of him, and he yelled, "Oh shit," leaping behind cover.

James managed to reach the building without drawing attention. He climbed up a ladder to the roof and approached the sniper slowly from behind when suddenly a second masked man tackled James from behind and pinned him to the ground.

James kicked him off and jumped to his feet. The sniper swung at him. James dodged behind and elbowed him in the back. Then they both charged at him. James blocked multiple swings, then punched one directly in the face and then kicked the other knocking him over.

James then grabbed the one. He punched and tossed him from the roof. He landed directly in front of Harvey, but then the other picked up James's gun and pointed it at him. James paused and raised his hands and spoke, "OK, let's both calm down. If you put down the gun, we can figure this out. OK?"

"Infernum diem," the attacker said.

James looked puzzled. The guy was shot in the back of the head from behind, and as his body feel, it revealed Harvey. James dropped his arms.

"Thanks."

"No problem, but next time, you call me fat I might decide to sit back and watch. Anyway, any idea why these guys started shooting at us?" Harvey asked.

James holstered his gun, "No, but before you…"

"Before I saved your ass…" Harvey interrupted.

"Yeah, before you 'saved my ass', the guy said something, but it… it wasn't English," James said.

"Well, do you remember what it was?" Harvey asked.

"Yeah, something like inferno… no… infernum… infernum diem… whatever that means…" James said.

"It's Latin," Harvey said.

"How the hell do you know that?" James asked.

"Hey, I'm not just a sexy body. I've also got a genius brain," Harvey said.

"Not since I've known you," James smiled and removed the attacker's mask and the gloves. Harvey stopped him and pointed at the attacker's neck.

"Look, do you know what that is?" he asked.

"A tattoo," James said.

"Very funny, but not just any tattoo. That is the tattoo every member of the Green family gets. They all have that tattoo onto them... even the children," Harvey said.

"But the Green family are gone. They were wiped out years ago," James said.

"Apparently, not all of them," Harvey said.

"Well, if they're really back, I don't think they'll take to lightly to the Spire family holding all of their old territories and businesses," James said.

"So, what you're saying is we've not only got a psychopathic murder on the loose, but we've also got a brewing gang war on our hands. That's just great how about an epidemic while we're at it, or maybe a couple natural disaster, really spice things up," Harvey said.

"Do you think this is the hell that Jason was warning us about?" James asked.

"Let's damn well hope so because I can't deal with more."

Chapter 9

George was sitting at a table with Anthony, Michael, Jason and many other high-ranking members of the family. He slammed the table in anger yelling.

"There still alive. Derrick, you assured me that there were no other members of the Green family left alive after the death of Henry Green. You swore to me."

Derrick started talking so quickly and nervously. He couldn't be understood.

"Jason, could you please…" George sighed.

Jason pulled out his gun and shot Derrick through the head. His head slammed into the table, and blood poured from it.

"Thank you, Jason, who seems to be the only GOD DAMN ONE OF YOU CAPABLE OF DOING THEIR JOB," George said.

"What? What have I done?" Michael said.

"Shut it, Michael. I'm not in the mood for your stupidity. Now we need to settle this. I will not allow them to return to regain control. We must extinguish them. Does anyone have a plan?" George shouted.

Anthony raised his hand.

"What is it, Anthony?" George asked.

"We could make a truce. We could return their territories and businesses to them and stop this war before one happens cease all bloodshed, avoid pointless fighting and save ourselves," Anthony said.

"Anybody else?" George shook his head.

Jason then raised his hand.

George nodded, "Yes, Jason."

"Now what we could do? A way for us to keep our strength... a way to defeat our enemy without giving up what we have gained from them," Jason said.

"Sounds great. I'm all ears," George said.

"We wait... wait for them to make a mistake... reveal themselves in the open, and when they do, we strike... we strike fast and hard, and we eliminate them all at once," Jason said.

George nodded his head, "Yes, you hear, do all of you useless idiots hear that? This one man has done more for us than all of you combined. I am ashamed of all of you. Thank you, Jason. I pick your plan."

"But, father, we will suffer great losses... losses we don't need to lose," Anthony said.

"And they will die for the greater good of the family," George said.

"Don't worry, I will lead the attack myself. We will not lose many," Jason added.

"Good... why are you all still sitting there? Everyone up... gather your forces... ready your men... arm your weapons... we are at war," George said.

Everyone rushed out.

George said, "Wait, Jason, I must speak with you."

Anthony stared at Jason as they left.

Once the last person left, George said, "Thank you."

"For what?" Jason asked.

"For everything… everything you have done for me… for the family… since the day I met you. You have done nothing but giving me your best. You have never failed me… never faltered. Your commitment and your loyalty is unmatched even by my own flesh and blood," George said.

"What are you saying?" Jason asked.

"Today, I would like to make it official. Jason, will you be my son?" George asked.

Jason looked stunned and said, "What about Anthony and Michael?"

"That's why I need you more than you can imagine. After I'm gone, the family will be handed to the three of you. I trust that together, you can all make it work. I trust you can protect them, teach them, mould them into better men. So, Jason, do you accept?" George sighed.

Jason paused before saying, "Of course. How could I say no?"

George smiled and hugged Jason.

Jason however looked disgusted but hugged him back.

"I… I'm sorry for that. Now go… go… finish the job," George said.

"Will do," Jason said and left.

Then Jason closed the door behind and saw Anthony standing in the hallway. He said, "Are you happy? You've sentenced hundreds to death."

"Oh, if only that were true. But, no, I have done what is necessary," Jason said.

Anthony shook his head, "You may have fooled everyone else, with your knight in shining armour portrayal, but I know what you really are."

"And what is that," Jason smiled and asked.

"A monster… you are a monster… nothing more… you don't care about the family… all you care about is…" Anthony said.

"Suffering! Good job, Anthony. You finally said it to my face… said what you've been holding inside all these years… took you long enough." Jason interrupted saying.

"I will be watching you, and when you make a mistake, however small, I will see it, and I will end you," Anthony said trying to intimidate Jason.

"Hahahahahaahahaha…" Jason laughed. "Oh, you think I'm afraid of you. I was born in the dark. I fear no one, but I can see in your eyes. I can see your fear I terrify you. See you later, Anthony."

Jason walked away from Anthony who stood there watching him leaving with rage in his eyes.

Chapter 10

James and Harvey were at the police station, "Infernum diem… infernum diem…"

"Can you stop talking to yourself? Some of us are actually trying to work," James said.

"Hey, I'm working. I just can't figure out what it means," Harvey said.

"Figure out what? What means?" James asked.

"What the guy said? You know infernum diem?" Harvey asked.

"It doesn't matter. He was probably saying something random. Just focus on finding the Green family," James said.

"Hey, Johnson, you're smart. You know what infernum diem means?" Harvey paused.

Johnson shook his head, "No, not a clue."

"Damn it, hey, James," Harvey called.

James now annoyed and replied, "What?"

"You know, you told me to look for the Green family?"

"Yes, I remember. It was about five seconds ago," James said.

"Well, I found them," Harvey said.

James jumped from his desk and rushed over to Harvey's desk.

"What? How?"

"Look, cameras picked up a large group of vehicles driving up to the old Green family farm, now unless that's just a massive coincidence," Harvey said pointing at his computer.

James shouted to the whole precinct, "Everyone, get ready. We found them… we found them."

All the cops started getting ready. Harvey and James started informing all the cops, "Alright, listen up. We are at the brink of a gang war. The Green family has returned, and reports show they've been hitting Spire family territories all over the city. So the plan is simple. We head to the old Green family farm and bring them back here and try to convince them to stop this war before it begins and prevent unneeded bloodshed. Do you all understand?" James said.

They all nodded.

"Then let's head out, ladies," Harvey shouted.

Jason walked down the street alone and said to himself, "I can't believe it. It's nearly time. After all these years of painful agonising repetition, finally it is going to be worth when I tear everything to the ground and can finally rest."

Jason saw a pizza delivery guy walking past him and knocking on a house saying, "Hello, did you order the double pepperoni?"

The guy at door answered, "Yeah, that's us. How much?"

The pizza guy replied, "That will be $19.9."

Bang… Jason shot the pizza guy in the back of the head and whipped the homeowner in the face with his pistol, then kicked him inside. His wife screamed.

Jason pointed the gun at her yelling, "SHUT UP, OR I SWEAR I'LL DO WORSE THAN SHOOT YOU."

"Take what you want. Just don't hurt us," the husband said.

Jason squatted down and stared at him, "But what I want is to hurt you, but don't worry, I've got use for you yet. Hahahaha…"

Anthony and Michael were at their favourite club. Michael was dancing and enjoying himself while Anthony was sitting alone stewing. Michael leaped into the seat opposite to him and spoke, "You should see it out there. It's exhilarating."

"Great, I'm happy for you," Anthony said very uncaringly.

"Ah… come on, man, don't be so glum. We should be celebrating," Michael said.

"Celebrating what exactly?" Anthony asked confused.

"Celebrating the end to the Green family, of course," Michael replied.

"You're just as delusional as father. Do you know how many we will lose doing this?" Anthony sighed.

Michael not caring answered, "So, that's their job. Their job is to die for us, and besides, you never know Jason might fail and you can become father's favourite again. That's what you want, isn't it?"

"No, something… something feels off. Jason seemed like he knew something," Anthony said.

"So, the guy's crazy. Who knows what's going on in that guy's head, and frankly, I don't want to know," Michael said.

"No, he seemed different almost excited," Anthony said.

"Are you not listening to me? The guy is mentally insane. Why wouldn't he be excited about the idea of killing," Michael said.

"No, it doesn't feel right," Anthony said and got up.

Michael said, "Hey, where are you going?"

"He's up to something. I know he is. I need to know what," Anthony said.

"Fine suit yourself. More booze for me," Michael sighed and started downing another bottle.

Anthony walked away.

"Jackass," he said to himself.

Anthony left the club and walked towards his car in the middle of the night, and he climbed inside and sighed and said to himself, "What are you up to?"

A voice replied, "Do you really want to know?"

Anthony grabbed his gun, but someone started strangling him from the back seat.

Jason said, "Sh… sh… sh… don't try to fight. You can't win."

Then Anthony went limp as he had passed out.

Jason leaped over to the front seat and started the car. He said to the unconscious Anthony, "I hope you're ready… ready for the end… ready for me to rip down your whole world. I have been waiting for this day for 12… no… 18 years… I can't wait for you to see it… see what I've been planning all these years… see the very thing you have suspected from me for so long… see that you were right all along and yet you still lost."

Jason was in his living room. It's night. He was listening to a calming guitar melody and danced while messing with a homemade device. Jacob and Izzy walked in and called, "Daddy."

"Yes, what is it?" Jason asked without turning around still playing with his device.

"Who are the strange people sitting in the dining room?" they asked.

Jason chuckled, "They… they are some friends of mine."

"Why are they tied up?" Izzy asked.

"Well, you see, these particular friends of daddy… they sleepwalk, and we wouldn't want them getting hurt, would we? Accidentally getting injured?" Jason answered.

"No, we wouldn't," she replied.

"See, now go back to bed. Tomorrow is going to be a very big day," Jason answered.

They walked out. Jason took a sip of his milk and continued dancing. Then he finished his device saying, "Tomorrow is your time to shine."

Tick… tick… boom… muffled screaming… Jason got up and entered the dining room. Both the couple from earlier and Anthony were there. Anthony was still knocked out, but the couple were wide awake.

Jason grabbed the wife's throat and said, "Shut the hell up. You're disrupting my kids sleep."

The husband made a muffled sound as well, so Jason removed his gag.

"You touch her, and I'll break every bone in your god damn body."

"Oh, that's so funny. You… you really think I'm scared. Oh, it's… that's just hilarious," Jason pretended to look scared. He burst out laughing.

The husband spat on Jason's face.

"Now that wasn't very good manners. Remember we're at the dinner table. I'm going to have to teach you a lesson," Jason said.

Jason put the gag back into the husband's mouth and plunged a fork into his hand. Jason then said, "Oh, now look, you've got me all worked up. How about a quick game?"

Jason grabbed the husband's hand and slammed it on the table grabbing a knife. The wife started crying.

Jason said, "Your familiar with five-finger fillet, right? If not, don't worry. I teach you along the way." Jason grabbed the husband's hand to keep it still and said, "Now if you move your fingers, I will play this game with your wife instead."

The husband looked back at his wife.

Jason said, "You wouldn't want that, would you?"

The husband shook his head.

Jason replied, "Good. Now the one rule is if you miss the gap between your hand, you may very well lose one of those fingers. You understand?"

The husband nodded.

Jason smashed the knife into the table in the gap between the husband's fingers and said, "PLAY."

The husband picked up the knife slowly and looked at his wife who was crying and shaking her head no. Jason saw this and grabbed another knife and held it against her throat and said, "Play or my floor will have a hint of red on it."

The husband took a deep breath and started playing.

Jason said, "Oh, one more thing. If you mess up three times, I will kill her without hesitation. OK. Now go."

The husband started playing. He does well for a while going at slow speed.

Jason said, "Faster."

The husband flinched as he went slightly faster.

Jason moved the knife along his wife's throat causing her to squeal and him to flinch and said, "I said faster."

The husband went a lot faster and ended up cutting a small part of his index finger. He groaned.

Jason said, "One life down. Again…"

The husband went again doing very well at a high speed.

Jason said, "FASTER."

The husband went at nearly full speed and instantly cut his thumb.

Jason said, "Oh, one to go. Now I want you to go at full speed for let's say 10… no… 15 seconds, and then I will leave you in peace."

The husband braced himself as he went. He mastered the game doing it perfectly.

Jason yelled, "And time."

The husband dropped the knife sweating in fear.

Jason removed the knife from the wife's throat and put it away. She sighed in relief.

Jason said, "Job well done. You're a very good husband, but I kind of wanted to see more so." Jason quickly grabbed the knife the husband was using and slammed it into the table once more… this time amputating the husband's ring finger.

The husband squirmed in pain. Jason picked the finger up and said, "What a nice ring! I truly enjoyed our game. See you in the morning. You've got a big day ahead of you."

Jason left the room as the wife was crying and the husband exhausted.

Chapter 11

James, Harvey and dozens of cops were driving to the Green family farm.

"Jim, what's the plan if things go sideways? You know if they don't feel like coming in quietly?" Harvey asked.

"That's simple. We don't let it go sideways," James said.

"Oh, great plan... really just the greatest plan... I've ever heard," Harvey said sarcastically. Then one of the cops started shaking.

"Hey, hey, buddy, are you alright?" James said.

"He's a rookie. This is his first time in the field like this," the cop next to him said.

"Hey, it's going to be OK. I'll watch your back out there. Alright?" James said to the scared rookie.

The rookie nodded his head as the driver in the front yelled, "We're here."

"Everyone, get ready, go... go... go..." James yelled.

They poured out of the vehicle along with dozens and dozens of others, and as they exited, dozens more people stood in the farm.

"Put your hands in the air now," Harvey yelled.

The cops all formed a perimeter around the mob members.

One member stepped forward saying, "Why should we? We have committed no crimes."

"Cut the bullshit. We know you've been attacking the Spire family," Harvey replied.

"With what evidence?" the man responded.

"Look, we're not here to arrest you," James lowered his gun and replied.

"Then why are you here?" the man said.

"To prevent a war. Now I'm sure you don't want a war... don't want unneeded bloodshed," James said.

"Maybe we do," the man interrupted.

"No, I know you don't. You've already suffered enough from the Spire family. You can't afford an all-out war," James said.

"How could you help us; you have no sway over them," the man said.

"Just come with us, and we can sort this all out, without any bloodshed," James said.

"Why should we trust you, a cop? How do I know this isn't a trap, and you actually work for the Spires?" the man asked.

"Everyone lowers your weapons," James stated.

"Jim, are you crazy?" Harvey yelled.

"Just do it. Trust me," James said.

Harvey reluctantly lowered his gun and was followed by all the others.

James said, "See, you can trust us."

The man paused and looked side to side at other members before answering.

"Very well, we will come with you, but if I sense anything at all, the deal's off."

"You have nothing to be worried about," James said. They load them up in armoured transport vehicles and began to drive.

Harvey said to James, "Something feels off."

"How so?" James asked.

"The Spires... why haven't they reacted they haven't done anything?" Harvey said.

"Maybe they don't want a war either," James said.

"Let's hope that's the reason," Harvey said.

Anthony woke up in a random abandoned factory and looked around and yelled, "Hello... is any one there? Hello..."

Jason emerged from the darkness, "You can call for help all you want... No one can hear you."

Anthony stared in disbelief, "You... what are you doing, Jason?"

"You already know... you've suspected it from the very beginning... since the moment we met. You never trusted me... And you were right," Jason said.

"So, all these years, just a lie," Anthony said.

"Yes, yeeeees... oh, it feels good to finally admit it. You have no idea how hard it is to keep a secret for 12 years... 12 years of lying... and deceit all leading up to this day... this moment," Jason answered.

"Are you going to kill me?" Anthony asked.

"Kill you? No, not yet. You see, I want you to watch," Jason said.

"Watch what?" Anthony asked.

"I want you to watch me burning everything you've ever known to the ground. I want you to watch as I rip away every fibre of your being piece by piece. I want you to feel every moment of it, and only then, after you have seen me rip your world apart in front of your eyes. Only then will you feel the sweet release of death," Jason smiled.

"You won't win. My father, he'll see through you. He'll stop you," Anthony said.

"You keep telling yourself that while I kill him in front of you," Jason said.

"IF YOU TOUCH HIM, I'LL KILL YOU… I'LL KILL YOU…" Anthony yelled.

Jason turned on a TV opposite to Anthony and spoke, "I hope you enjoy the show."

Anthony screamed out at Jason.

Jason walked away leaving a bomb in front of Anthony.

Chapter 12

The police transports were reaching the centre of the city. They were stuck in heavy traffic. Harvey beeped the horn yelling, "Come on, police business make way... make way..."

Not far down the street is Jason. He had tied the couple from earlier inside a car and strapped home-made explosives around the car.

"Please it's not too late," the man said.

"Ha... not too late you say... if only you knew how late it is... Have a nice ride," Jason said. He dropped a brick on the accelerator as the car jolted forward.

James and Harvey were sitting in one of the vehicles. James grabbed Harvey saying, "Isn't that car going a bit fast? Give me the binoculars."

James grabbed the binoculars and looked through seeing the driver was tied up and shouted, "Get out of the way. Everyone get out th—"

Boom... the car collided with one of the transports exploding causing cars to fly over the street. James and Harvey's car had its windows blown open, and they stumbled out into the smoke and fire.

James yelled out as he walked past bodies eventually reaching a group of survivors... a mix of cops and Green members. James said, "Is there anyone else? Did you see any other survivors?"

Gun shots were fired towards them. They all dived behind cover. James looked over and saw a dozen or so men in gas masks, fully equipped with battle gear and assault rifles marching down the street, and in front of them all is Jason not wearing a mask.

James jumped up opening fire at Jason, but Jason grabbed a random civilian from a car, blocking the bullets. A gun fight ensued. Two cops were shot and killed. James and the others fired back causing the Spire soldiers to disperse. James while ducking travelled through the sea of cars. He came up to the side of a Spire soldier firing over the hood of a car.

James stood to fire and shot him through the head. A storm of bullets sprayed all around James. He ran and leaped behind a van as the bullets kept on coming. Jason popped up and hit a Green member in the head. A cop tackles Jason into a car, but Jason kicked the cop back into another car, then grabbed the cop and smashed his head through a car window and pushed his head down impaling his throat on a shard of glass.

Then pulling back out his gun, he shot the Green family member in the head. Another cop fired at Jason. He rolled underneath a car, and the cop walked closer to see where he went. Jason from underneath a car shot the cop in the ankle, dropping him to the ground, and then shot the cop in the head as he rolled back out into the open.

A Spire soldier turned the corner, and James jumped out the way dodging the shot, then raised his gun but had it kicked from his hands. James then tackled the soldier causing wild bullet spray. The soldier turned and smashed James into a car. James got up, and the soldier drew a knife.

The soldier swung several times, but James dodged each swing and finally grabbed the soldiers knife hand and punched him with his other hand multiple times before kicking him into a car, causing him to drop the knife. James dived for it, but so does the soldier. Pulling James away, they both pushed each other away. The soldier pinned James to a car and began to strangle him.

"James," Harvey yelled. He tossed the knife at James who caught it and plunged it into the soldier's throat. James then ran towards Harvey sliding over the roof of a car kicking another soldier over before stabbing him repeatedly in the chest.

Back to Jason, he who using his martial arts disarmed four cops before pulling out a knife and stabbing them all. Suddenly, James tackled Jason to the ground and smashed his face on the ground, into the dirty tarmac roads, but Jason headbutted James knocking him backwards. Jason rose to his feet and took several swings. Some blocked, but most landed on James, which eventually stunned him. Jason then threw James over a car. James landed with the other survivors. They are completely surrounded by Spire soldiers.

"Line them up," Jason yelled.

The Spire soldiers lined them all up.

"Why are you listening to him? He's crazy. He'll probably kill you after this," Harvey yelled.

"You really think I would kill my own men because your right?" Jason replied and fired his gun killing all the Spire soldiers and all Green family members.

James, Harvey and all the other cops looked stunned, shocked and confused. Jason threw his gun down, got on his knees and raised his hands saying, "I surrender."

The cops ran towards him and arrested him. Jason stared directly at James as he was loaded into a SWAT van.

James said to Harvey, "What's he playing at? Why did he kill his own men and surrender?"

"I don't know, but we've been chasing this bastard for the last decade. So I know whatever the reason it ain't good," Harvey answered.

"But why now? Why stop? Why give up, after serving them for 12 years? Why now betray them?" James asked.

"He's crazy, Jim. Men like that don't have reasons," Harvey said.

Jason was sitting in interrogation with James sitting opposite. They were sitting in complete silence until Jason said, "It's good to see you again. It's been so, so long since I've seen you in person, too long."

James slammed the table yelling, "You don't talk unless asked. Do you understand?"

"I understand… Officer," Jason smirked replying.

"Tell me, why did you surrender?" James asked.

"I have seen the error of my ways… the horrible things I have done. I know now that they were wrong, so very wrong, and I wish to make it right," Jason answered.

"Make it right? How?" James asked.

"I'm so glad you asked. I have more than enough evidence to put the entire Spire crime family behind bars for more than life," Jason replied.

James looked shocked and asked, "And what's in it for you? Why give up the money and power?"

"Now that, that's the good part. We both get what we want. You get to put an end to the largest crime family in the state. You become a hero… a SAINT, and crime takes a dive, and all you have to do is let one man go," Jason smiled saying.

"That's not happening. No. You've killed too many. You're not getting off free. You will pay for what you've done, every last thing," James now angrily said.

"We will see… we will see, my friend," Jason chuckled.

The commissioner entered and spoke, "James, can I speak with you?"

James reluctantly left as Jason waved at him goodbye. They left and entered the opposite side of the one-way glass. They stood facing each other, and in the middle is Jason.

"So, what did you want to talk about, sir?" James asked.

"I don't know how to tell you this," the commissioner replied.

"Tell me what?" James asked.

"I'm sorry, James, but we're taking it," the commissioner sighed replying.

"Are you kidding me? After everything he's done… everyone he has killed… taken… broken… and you're just gonna let him walk away?" James yelled.

When they were talking, someone brought Jason a glass of milk.

"Look, I know the horrors he's done. Alright. Trust me, I've spent nights just like you looking over his case files studying him, trying to get justice for everyone he has hurt… but the Spire crime family have done 10 times the damage, hurt 10 times the people and are 10 times worse than him," the commissioner said.

"No no… they're not… they don't kill for no reason. He does… he is not a man. If we let him go, it would be no different than unleashing a hungry lion into a crowd of people. We would kill hundreds," James yelled back.

"This isn't up for further discussion. The papers are already being drawn up. I'm sorry, James, but this is the right decision, and besides, you should be happy. His case will no longer sit rotting on your desk," the commissioner replied.

The commissioner left. James stood stunned and furious. Then he turned and looked at Jason. He took a sip of his milk and stared directly at James… almost like he could see through the one-way glass. James exited and went up to Harvey and said, "I need you to buy me some time."

"Buy you time? For what?" Harvey asked.

"I'm going back in to question him," James said.

"Why? What's the point? The commissioner has already made his mind up," Harvey said.

"I just… I need to know… to know why? Why he's done all of this. Please, Harvey," James said.

"Fine, but you owe me one," Harvey said.

"Thank you," James said.

Harvey distracted to guards in front of the interrogation room as James sneaked back in to the interrogation room and broke the camera.

"Ah… good… I wasn't finished with our little chat either," Jason said.

James sat down and threw Jason's milk into a wall.

"Rude," Jason said.

"Shut up… tell me, why did you do it? Why did you do all of it?" James aggressively asked.

Jason smiled.

"Good question… you can finally get your answers… get to finally scratch the itch that's been nagging you for over a decade. I suggest you savour every moment of this. Why did I do it? I did it because… because why not. Ever since I was a mere child I saw the world for what it truly was. I saw the sickness hidden underneath everyone and everything's skin.

"I saw how everyone conformed to the same routine day after day after day after day, how nothing ever changed, how all we do is live a faded copy of our ancestors lives, living it on repeat until we eventually die, shrivel up and rot… So I decided to change, to be different, to break the cycle and to cure myself of the sickness. Everyone I have killed has been cured from the sickness. Everyone who I have released from their pointless lives of repetition has been cured. So, in reality, I'm no killer. I'm a healer."

"So you chose to become this thing, to become a monster?" James asked.

"No… no… no… NO… I didn't choose it. It chose me. You see every now and then the world spits a monster out: Genghis Kahn, Adolf Hitler, Joseph Stalin. I'm just the next in line. I made a sacrifice. You see, everyone wants to be the hero of the story, the knight in shining armour, but at the end of the day, someone has to be the villain," Jason laughed.

"But why? Why kill so many innocents? why cause so much suffering?" James asked.

"BECAUSE THIS WORLD, IT DOESN'T CARE ABOUT YOU… it only cares about making the rich richer and the poor poorer, another case of its putrid repetition and conformity, so I arose to set it all aflame, to end the misery of this hell hole," Jason answered.

James didn't speak.

Jason continued, "You know, I remember all my victims. I keep little scrap books on all of them. My first though, you never forget my first, you know him, little Marcus... oh little Marcus... he was my school bully... the one who followed the rules of conformity. He fit in to society, repeating the life of so many before him. He tortured me; everybody did; not a moment of my life wasn't met by excruciating suffering; and one day, when I was 12, I had enough.

"I wanted him to suffer like I had for so... so long. So I fought back, and I sunk my teeth into his throat and ripped it wide open, and he collapsed to the dirty muddy ground gurgling on his own blood begging god for mercy, barely able to breathe. I pulled a rock from my pocket and swung again and again and again until he was unrecognisable, and I enjoyed it... every moment of it.

"If I could go back, I wouldn't do it again. Instead, I would make him suffer a lot... lot more... After I killed him, I took the evidence and hid it all away. I thought I had done it. The police your own partner didn't suspect me at all, except my principal did. He knew how Marcus treated me... how he tortured me... how he didn't care because he saw me just like everybody else... a freak, and he knew it was me, so I snuck into his office and poured homemade poison into his coffee, and once he drank it, it burnt through HIS THROAT (Jason slammed the table).

"Then after that, it was as simple as copying his handwriting onto a suicide letter where he admitted to killing Marcus, and I had done it, gotten away with murder, and it was good, watching them suffer. So I did it again and again... each time more inventive and painful than the last."

James looked sick. "How many lives have you taken?" he asked.

"I never lost count. I remember every single one of them... 497 and counting, although some were larger enough to count as two. Hahahah..." Jason grinned wider than ever before.

"You think this is funny?" James asked.

"Oh... but that's the point. It is funny. It's a joke... all one big long painful excruciating joke... but do you want to hear my favourite, the kill that holds a special place in my heart? Of course, you do. Look at yourself you love it. Alright, here we go.

"His name was Cecil Moore. He was an ordinary man nothing special about him. He was a security guard working at the docks, and one night, he caught me drowning another one of my victims, and this, it infuriated me because you see I had made a mistake all my years of precise planning, and yet I had done something so many of you do... so many of you close-minded, ordinary fools, and it made me very, very angry.

"I knocked him out and screamed at myself for making such a mistake. So I wanted to make sure I never made another. I took my knife and carved the words, failure into my arm (as he said that last part, he mimicked doing it, pretending to carve it into his arm) as a constant reminder of my mistake and what would happen if I ever made another.

"Now, of course, I'm still very upset with myself. So I thought to cheer myself up. I thought long and hard about how to make this man suffer... suffer with me like never before... And then it came to me. Can you guess what it was... mummification? It was perfect... so... so perfect.

109

"I wrapped him head to toe in bandages and placed him neatly into a box and trust me it wasn't easy. He just wouldn't stop wiggling and struggling. Then I poured a dozen or so rats, which I had starved for days into the box with him, and the final touch a camera, so I could watch my creation, watch as they slowly ripped him apart and feasted on his pathetic worthless flesh. Sometimes, I still watch that video, and I pretend his screams are an orchestra and I the conductor," Jason said. Jason started imitating an orchestra while singing Ava Marie.

"You're sick... you're insane," James said.

Jason stopped, "Ah... you see, the interesting thing is, technically, technically, I'm not insane. You see because the definition of insanity is doing the same thing over and over again and expecting a different result, but out of the two of us in this room, only you fill that quota because I may do the same thing over and over again. But I don't expect a different result.

"I do it expecting the same result... death and suffering, while you follow the rules of conformity... of repetition... and you also arrest and arrest hoping you will make a difference... make the world a better place... and personally, I don't think you've succeeded. Do you? So, in reality, who's really insane? Hahahahahahahaha..."

"Why now? Why betray the family now?" James asked.

"They have become futile; I have used them for all their worth, and now they are nothing," Jason responded.

"And you just stabbed them in the back after all these years? Don't you care about anyone... anything?" James asked.

"Listen, Jim, when the world turns, it's back on you. They tell you to turn your back on the world, but I didn't. Instead, when the world turned its back on me, I stabbed it in the back. To me, you're already all dead," Jason smiled.

"So you murdered innocents for no reason other than your sick own personal problems," James looked revolted.

"None of them are innocent. We have all sinned... even you detective... Tell me, how's the wife?" Jason said.

"Don't you speak about her," James got defensive.

"What? But I got on so well with Amanda," Jason said.

"Don't say her name. You don't get to say it," James said getting aggressive.

"It's been a while, hasn't it? Tell me, has her hand healed yet?" Jason smirked.

"Shut up," James yelled.

"Why? I'm only saying words. Words can't hurt anyone, can they? What about your son, or the new one coming? I'm feeling it will be a girl," Jason sighed.

"DON'T YOU DARE," James yelled.

"Dare what? What do you think I'm gonna do? Because I will do whatever it is, I'm sure I've done worse," Jason said.

James pulled out his gun and pointed it at Jason yelling, "SHUT UP... SHUT THE HELL UP..."

"Go on... do it. Rip away your life... rip yourself from your family's lives. (Jason leaned forward so the gun was against his forehead.) Do it, Jim... avenge everyone I have hurt... everyone I have killed," Jason said.

James held the gun firm as he questioned doing it.

"DO IT... DO IT, JIM. END MY SUFFERING... END EVERYONE'S SUFFERING... PULL THE TRIGGER...

GO ON… DO IT… DO IT… END THIS NOW… DO IT…
DO IT…" Jason exploded.

James crunched his face as he pulled the trigger, but no
bullet was fired. James looked confused as Jason leaned back
in his chair laughing, "Hahahahahahaha…"

"How I?" James asked.

Jason threw the ammo clip onto the table. James checked
and saw. It was the one from his handgun.

"Congratulation, Jim. You had the guts to ruin your own
life. Leave your wife alone. Take away your kids childhood
all to stop me… all for me… I'm flattered… really I am… to
think I have broken you. And, without even really trying to,"
Jason said.

James stormed out. Jason laughed once again. James
entered the main precinct and rushed over to his desk where
he sat down completely broken as tears slowly dripped from
his face. On seeing this, Harvey hurried over and comforted
James asking, "What the hell happened in there, Jim? Jim, tell
me what that psycho said? Look, whatever it is, don't listen
to him. He's not stable. It was a lie… it was…"

"But wasn't a lie. He was telling the truth… every word,"
James interrupted.

"Hey, it's OK. You can tell me. Now what did he say?"
Harvey asked.

"He… he said… he said he had broken me… overtaken
me," James said.

"Well, that's a lie. It's obviously a lie. He's just trying to
get under your skin," Harvey said.

"I tried to shoot him," James shook his head.

"You what?" Harvey got shocked and said, "I… I… I…
he just wouldn't stop. He just kept pushing… aaa… and

pushing. He kept mentioning them, Harvey: Amanda... the kids... He just... he wouldn't stop, so pulled out my gun... and he begged for it... he... he wanted it... kept telling me to end the suffering. So I... I pulled the trigger..." James said nearly broken in sadness.

"And," Harvey asked.

"He had removed the magazine. He broke me, Harvey," James said and began to fully breakdown.

"That son of a bitch," Harvey said.

Harvey ran over to the interrogation room. James tried to stop him, and several guards also tried to stop him, but he pushed through them entering the room. When guards tried to hold him back, he yelled, "YOU SICK BASTARD... YOU SAY ANYTHING ABOUT MY PARTNER AGAIN, I SWEAR I WONT HESITATE. YOU HEAR ME... I'LL KILL YOU... I'LL KILL YOU AND SHOW YOU REAL SUFFERING."

Harvey kept trying to walk further in.

Jason stood up and smiled, "Real suffering... suffering was born with me and will die with me. It is an infection, and you will all catch it. I am unstoppable. I am an ever constant."

Harvey yelled. He was removed from the room, and Jason waved him goodbye as the door was closed in Harvey's face.

Chapter 13

Jason was in the commissioner's office. Harvey and James knocked on the door, and the commissioner opened it and closed it behind him. He said, "Yes, Detectives."

"Let us in," James said.

"And why in the world would I do that? Not only did you sneak into question him even more, but also you burst into the room and threatened to kill him. So tell me why should I let you in?" the commissioner asked.

"Because we know him better than anyone," Harvey said.

"We know him front and back, everything about him," James added.

"So he is giving us information. We don't need an expert, or two," the commissioner explained.

"Then do it for me," James spoke.

"What?" the commissioner said.

"And do it for me, too," Harvey said.

"We deserve to be in there sir. We have spent over a decade hunting this son of a bitch down. We deserve to be in there, so I ask you, let us in," James added.

The commissioner hesitated for a moment.

"Fine, but if either of you two lose your cool, you will leave the room immediately. Do you understand?"

"Yes, sir," they both said. They entered the office. Harvey and James took their seats.

"Sorry for keeping you waiting," the commissioner said.

"No problem at all. I'm in no rush, and besides, I'm very, very patient," Jason said.

"So what evidence do you have on the Spires then?" the commissioner asked.

"I have audio and video recordings of each and every high-ranking member... both committing and admitting to multiple major crimes, but the big one... oh, you are going to love the big one. I have a recording of every single member plotting the attack on the city centre, which tragically occurred this morning and took the lives of countless innocents and officers alike... such a tragedy!" Jason answered.

"A tragedy you were a part of," Harvey said.

"Harvey," the commissioner said annoyed.

"No, it's quite alright, Detective. I am here to help you put a stop to these... these savages, and I may have been a part of this tragic event, but I can assure you that I only did it for me and my family's safety," Jason said.

Harvey and James looked infuriated.

Jason said, "Please commissioner continue..."

"Alright, now once you hand us this information, your life will be in danger. Even after we arrest the family, your safety cannot be fully assured, so we will put you in witness protection. You will be relocated to a different country and given a new identity. Do you understand this?" the commissioner said.

Jason looked at James and said, "I understand."

"Now what are all of your demands?" the commissioner asked.

"Full pardon for all crimes… both known and unknown… and I want to take my son and daughter with me," Jason said.

"You have children?" James asked.

"What mad woman would have a child with you?" Harvey asked.

"DETECTIVES…" the commissioner said.

"That's very impolite of you, Detectives. How would you like it if I spoke about your family," Jason added.

Jason stared at James and gave him a smug look.

"OK, then, where is this evidence?" the commissioner asked. Jason pulled out a USB drive. "Right here is all you need to bring them down forever to crumble the Spire family empire into nothing more but a bad memory," Jason stated.

"OK then. Until your new identity is ready, you will have a police escort with you while we raid the Spire home and…" the commissioner said.

"If I may interrupt, I would not like an escort," Jason interrupted.

"Are you sure? We cannot ensure your safety without one," the commissioner said.

"I am sure, and I would like to be present at the raid. I would like to say goodbye to my former employers before they pay for their terrible crimes," Jason said.

"If we do that, your life will be at high risk. So are you sure?" the commissioner asked.

"Don't worry about me, Commissioner. I have a very particular set of skills to protect me (he looked at Harvey and James), and I am sure these fine detectives won't let anything happen to me," Jason said.

"Very well, we'll give you 15 minutes to speak with them before we go in," the commissioner said.

The commissioner left the room.

"If, for a second, I see no one is watching, I will put a bullet in you and blame it on the Spires. I hope you know that," Harvey said.

"Oh, I'm sure you will, Detective Harvey. I'm sure you will. Now, if you don't mind, I have to pick a suit for my last day of work. I'm thinking something new," Jason smiled and left the room.

"I still don't believe it. After everything that monster has done, he's just going to walk away... walk away facing no punishment for everything he has done," James said.

Harvey placed his hand on James's shoulder and said, "Sometimes, the good guys don't always win. Come on, let's try and focus on the Spires for now."

"Yeah... yeah... sure, Harvey, sure," James said in disbelief.

Chapter 14

A group of police were surrounding a car. Dozens more were around ready for a raid. James and Harvey walked past. The two officers guarding the van talked. "Do you know who we're guarding?" one asked.

"What they didn't tell you?" the other asked.

"No, they don't tell me anything," the other replied.

"Well, maybe if you listened... huh... we're guarding Jason Mitchells," the other said.

"Jason Mitchells, who's that?" the other asked. Harvey stopped and turned to them.

"You're new, aren't you?" he asked the last guard.

"Sir, yes, sir," he replied.

"Well, let me tell you about the thing you're guarding. He is no man. He is a monster... a pure evil beast. He has no remorse... no filter. He doesn't care who he kills. All he wants is to make it hurt as much as humanly possible, so that... that is who Jason Mitchells is. And don't ever forget," Harvey said.

Harvey walked away as the two guards were shaking in fear.

"Alright, we ready told him to come out," the commissioner said.

The guards hesitated. One reluctantly knocked on the door, and Jason exited walking towards the horde of cops wearing a pristine suit.

"You have 10 minutes, and we're going in," James said.

"I was promised 15, but 10 will do… Oh, don't look so glum, James. You won, but never ever forget… never ever forget the only reason you won is because I let you," Jason replied.

Jason walked towards the mansion. James stared at him in anger. Jason entered, and all the Spire family's high ranking members were there except for Anthony.

"Oh, thank god, you're alive, Jason? We were worried. Well, how did it go?" George asked.

"They're dead. The Green family is no more. Rejoice you have won," Jason replied.

They all cheered.

"I knew you could do it, Jason. You have never failed me, and I'm sure you never will," George said.

"I don't fail, George. I never fail," Jason answered.

"Does anyone know where Anthony is? I haven't heard from him since last night," Michael enquired.

"Oh, you know your brother. He's never been fond of Jason. He's probably sulking at home, sulking that Jason has once again out done him," George said.

"Yeah, you're probably right," Michael said.

"Jason, we must acknowledge this achievement… a toast. Shall we? Bring out the drinks…" George said.

"Ah… finally," Michael said.

Waiters brought bottles of champagne to everyone, except Jason who has a glass of milk.

"Ah, you remembered," Jason said.

"How could I forget, son? Everybody… everybody, can I have your undivided attention? Thank you. Today, we celebrate… we celebrate the defeat of our enemies… the scum that they are. Our family only grows bigger and stronger each passing day, and most of it is all thanks to one man, and one man alone.

"Here's to a man who, since the day I met him in that park, has served the family with all his efforts never once failing or giving me any reason to doubt him. Here's to Jason," George toasted.

They all drank and cheered for Jason.

"Speech… speech," Michael said.

"Alright… alright… Hello, everyone. As you know, I am Jason," Jason said. (They all cheered.) "Thank you… thank you. Now I have served the family for over a decade, and in that time, we have accomplished some truly great things together… things many only dream of. I have had a great time with you all… helping you all build this empire up together, but… but there is one last thing I must accomplish."

"And what's that?" George asked.

Jason had a long pause. He looked around at everybody's ecstatic faces and finally broke the silence and said, "Your destruction."

The police barged in and started handcuffing everyone.

"No get off me. Jason, what's happening. Help me… help Michael… JASON HELP US!" George screamed.

"No no. I don't think so," Jason said.

Jason walked away as George shouted, "NOOO, HOW COULD YOU, JASOOOOOOOON. I TRUSTED YOU, JASOOOOOOOOOOOOON."

Chapter 15

James and Harvey were at a party where the commissioner spoke. "Here is too us. Today, we put away the entire Spire crime syndicate only one got away. Let us celebrate this success."

Everyone cheered and started partying, except James and Harvey.

"I can't believe they're acting like we won. The only winner is him... that monster," James said to Harvey.

"It's time to let go, Jim. We've been chasing him for over a decade. It's over. I'm sorry to tell you that the hero doesn't always win, only in fairy-tales is that the case," Harvey said.

"Here's to all the people that psychopath killed, in hope they can rest in peace," James toasted.

"To the fallen," Harvey said as they both drank.

Then Officer Johnson walked up to them and asked, "Hey, Harvey, James."

"Hey, Johnson, how are you doing?" they both replied.

"I'm good, but I'm wondering are you still wondering about that Latin phrase," Johnson said.

"Sure, why not hit me?" Harvey said.

"Well, it took some research, but the phrase infernum diem roughly translates to Hell day. Does that mean anything to you?" Johnson asked.

Harvey and James looked at each other. They realised, flashing back to when Jason said hell is coming and when the shooter said infernum diem.

"That son of bitch," Harvey said.

"We've been playing this game all along," James said.

"Is something wrong?" Johnson said.

"No, just give us a moment," Harvey said.

Johnson walked away.

"Harvey, this has all been his plan," James said.

"Yeah, but what did hell mean, the road attack?" Harvey asked.

"No no. Something else... something bigger... Harvey," James said. "When are the Spire family being transported?"

"Right now, why?" Harvey asked.

"He's gonna kill them. That's his target," James said.

"Oh shit," Harvey said.

They both rush out of the party and towards their car.

Chapter 16

The prison transport was cruising along with the entire Spire Syndicate riding in the back. One of the guards said while they feasted on fast food.

"So… what are you doing tomorrow?"

"Probably going to the gym… work on my guns… What about you?" the driver responded.

"Yeah, I'll… wait what the hell is that?" the guard asked.

At the end of the night-fallen street, Jason stood holding an RPG. He fired it ripping the transport apart, tearing it to pieces. Boom… the transport crashed and caught on fire. Several of the cars exploded. Jason dropped the RPG and walked through the flames.

One guard tried to stand but was instantly shot by Jason. When another one ran towards him, Jason threw his gun and fought with his fists. The guard threw a left-side punch, but Jason blocked the strike and headbutted the guard. Then Jason grabbed the guard and headbutted him again and again and again until he dropped the guard who was coughing up blood.

Jason smashed the guards head in with his foot. Jason then wiped the blooded foot on the guards body and moved forward through the flames reaching the main transport and entered into it. Everyone was dead, except for George.

"MICHAEL... MICHAEL... PLEASE ANSWER ME. MICHAEL..." George was shouting.

"He can't hear you. He's dead, just like everyone else," Jason said.

"You... you traitor. I thought you were loyal... loyal to me... to us... to the family," George said.

"Loyal... LOYAL... I was never loyal to you... to the family... to the syndicate... You see, I didn't do it for the money, or the power, or the respect. No. I did it because I wanted to inflict as much pain and suffering as I could.

"Why do you think I amassed such a high body count? Because I wanted to. And just so you know I didn't betray the family to save my own skin or anything like that. No. I did it because I wanted to... I wanted to watch your empire... the empire I helped you build... burn. I wanted to watch it burn to the ground." Jason laughed and said "What, why," George said.

"NO... YOU STILL DON'T UNDERSTAND, do you? I've been behind it from the very beginning. You didn't stumble on to me in that park, George. You didn't discover me. I had been watching you... studying you... and I knew you would be in that park at that time... on that day.

"But that's not all. The ball where several members were poisoned... it was me. Well, it was also Henry Green. But I placed the dominos. He just knocked them over. Don't you remember? You put your poor excuse for a life form son, Michael, here in charge of booze for the party, but you know, Michael... the party animal... the failure, he forgot about champagne, so he asked me to get some, and so I anonymously gave the order to the Green family aka Henry Green.

124

"And then I leaked the information that you helped kill his son and so understandably pissed. He poisoned the champagne, but that's not all, those so-called Green family that returned aren't really part of the Green family. They were hired mercenaries. You see I have been in control the whole time manipulating everyone and everything, you... the police... the Greens... all part of my plan.

"I've killed and done a lot in my life, but this... this is my diamond... my magnum opus... my greatest achievement," Jason said. And he continued, "And you see, George, you've always seen yourself as the king of the chess board, and you're not wrong you are, but... but... but... BUT... I am the one behind the chess board... the one playing... the one controlling the game... moving you all around like just how I want you, and as they say to win chess sacrifices must be made, and you, George, you're the king. So you are the last sacrifice of this game."

"Why? Why are you like this?" George coughed.

"BECAUSE I'M THE ONLY ONE WHO SEES THE TRUTH... sees the rot... the sickness... the disease of this world... the mistake that is humanity... The world agrees... the world wants us dead... and every now and then. When the world settles, it throws a stone at us to simply rid itself of humanity. I saw this truth, and that is what I have done. I am the stone, here to cause suffering. I'm not just a man or a monster. I'm an idea a philosophy, a legacy.

"Tomorrow, after my pardon goes through forgiving me of all crimes, I will release a website discussing, describing, in detailed words and pictures of all of my victims, and it will act as my biography... my own bible if you will, and some day, someone will see it... someone with the power to do so much more than I ever could, and they will burn the world to the ground. When the smoke clears and everyone is dead and conformity is dead, they will place a gun to their head and pull the trigger, wiping the sickness of humanity from the planet. It's a shame you and I won't be there to see it. Once the disease is driven from it… once the repetition of mankind is gone… once all that remains… is suffering," Jason responded.

"You… you were like a son to me," George said.

"Oh, I know, George, and I don't blame you. In the disgust of humanity, your sons are near the bottom, but at least Anthony saw through me the entire time. Plus he's the only one who got away. For now, you see, he is watching us. I have him tied to a chair watching this through this body cam right here. He is watching his world burn around him… Now, my friend, this… this is goodbye. I won't miss you," Jason said.

Jason poured gasoline over George and said lastly, "Now, you suffer with me." Before tossing a match on him, Jason slowly walked away from the fire. George screamed in agony yelling in pure rage and suffering, "YOU'LL BURN FOR THIS. YOU'LL BURN IN HELL."

Anthony is still tied to the chair. As he watched his father burn, he screamed in sadness and dismay. As he saw the bomb in front of him near 0, Anthony tossed and turned. His father's screams pierced his ears. Finally, he freed himself.

Anthony sprinted towards a window as the bomb hit 0. Boom… the bomb exploded pushing Anthony out of the window as he fell several floors and landed on the ground. he screamed in pain and slowly crawled away saying, "Father… brother… I will avenge you… I promise, father, he will burn… he will burnnn… burn in hell."

Chapter 17

James and Harvey were driving through the dark streets. James said, "Come on, come on, come... where is it?"

"They can't be far," Harvey said.

"Oh, my god," James said.

"What? What is it?" Harvey asked.

James slowed down as he pointed out the front window.

Harvey turned and saw it. He saw the transports destroyed burning.

"No no, it can't be..." Harvey said.

James ran out of the car. Harvey followed him shouting, "Jim, JIM, slow down."

They reached the wreckage and walked through it, looking at the carnage.

"This can't be happening," James said. He saw the main transport and ran towards it.

Harvey followed. James climbed into the back where he and Harvey saw the burnt prisoners.

"He burnt them. He worked side by side with them for so many years, and he just burnt them," Harvey said.

James looked defeated.

"He won; he won, Harvey."

"No, we can still get him. It's not over," Harvey said.

"Yes, it is. He won't have left any evidence behind. FACE IT. He's been playing with us since the very beginning… since we walked into that woman's home and picked up that stupid letter. He didn't win today. He won all those years ago. We lost, Harvey. We lost," James said.

Harvey now too looked completely defeated.

"I'm sorry, Jim," he said…

"For what?" James asked.

"For allowing you to carry this weight, it will never leave you. Now, trust me, I would know. Come on, let's call it in," Harvey said.

Harvey walked out of the vehicle. James stayed inside for a few moments and looked at George's scorched corpse. He said, "As much as a monster he is, you still deserved this. You made a deal with the devil." James climbed out and walked back through the carnage. Police sirens lighted up his face.

The next day, Jason was walking through the woods once again, along with Jacob and Izzy. "Where are we going?" Jacob asked.

"I thought you should see it before we leave." Jason replied.

"See what?" Izzy asked.

"See where it all begun," Jason said.

They kept walking. They arrived at Jason's old house… his parents' house… as it is still half destroyed.

Jason said, "There it is… home sweet home."

"What happened, daddy?" Jacob asked.

"That is a story for another time, a story full of triumph and suffering. I'll tell it to you one day. Stay here. Would you? I wish to say goodbye one last time," Jason said.

Jason walked further forward as Jacob and Izzy stayed. Jason walked through the half-blown door. He smiled examining every inch of the home, running his hands along the walls. He explored the whole home. In his room, he picked up a half-burnt book... the same book his father would read to him when he was young.

Jason said, "I did it father. I overcame the monsters. They all run from me now."

Jason dropped the book as he left the home and walked through the forest. He stumbled upon the rock...the same rock he used to kill Marcus and his father. He picked it up and said, "Hello, old friend. I've missed you."

He continued walking and stumbled across his stick home. He smiled and said, "Now I am truly home. Ah... the memoires flooding back." Jason crawled inside.

He sat and looked at all his old drawings and said, "I have come so far since I constructed you, so many have joined me in my suffering. But none... none will ever compare to you. Marcus, my first and greatest. There isn't a day where I don't think of you, you haunt me, or I haunt myself. I would like to thank you... thank you for everything you did to me, the beatings... the humiliation... the mental breakage... everything because, without it, I may have never become who I am today.

"The truth is, Marcus, it was you... you are the monster... you created me... you made me this... you made me see the world. I hope you can hear me... hear everything I've done... see everyone I have killed... because the truth is I didn't kill them. You did. You made me suffer so now the world suffers with me. I want you to know that to know what you did and what you have done. Your torment will never end even in death… even in mine. You will rest knowing what you caused…"

Jason placed the rock down and crawled outside of the stick house and ignited a match. He said, "The suffering has only just begun." He flung the match at the wood as the home burnt. Jason walked away as the drawings crippled up.

Harvey, James and the commissioner were at a private airport. James and Harvey were off to the side. Harvey said to James, "I can't believe we're just letting him go. You know it's not too late, Jim. We can finish this here and now. Are you with me?"

"No, Harv. No, I'm not," James said.

"What I know is you want this bastard dead, even more than I do," Harvey said.

"You're right. I don't just want him dead. I want to pull him apart. I want him to suffer like all his other victims… experience everything they felt… But that is what he wants. He wants us to kill him because, if we do, the cycle continues, and we suffer more," James said.

"What if I do it? Not you… just me…" Harvey said.

"Harvey?" James said.

"You've got a family, and I don't. I have no one to miss me… no one to mourn me…" Harvey said.

"But you do. I'll miss you. Amanda will miss you. Your god kids will miss you…" James said.

"My god kids? Are you being serious?" Harvey asked.

"Did I stutter?" James asked.

Harvey hugged James and spoke, "Thank you, brother."

Then a car pulled up. Harvey said, "Then I guess it's time to finally let go."

"So it is," James said.

Jason, Jacob and Izzy exited the car. Jason said to Izzy and Jacob, "Wait here a moment. Daddy's got to say goodbye to some old friends."

Jason walked towards Harvey and James. He smiled and said, "So did you figure it out yet, infernum diem. Hell day."

"Yeah, we figured it out," Harvey said.

"Not quick enough, though, apparently, but I wouldn't dwell on them. They were all criminals, thrives, murderers and much, much worse. They deserved to suffer," Jason said.

"And what about all the innocents… all the normal people you slaughtered?" James asked.

"You just answered your own question there. They were normal nobodies just like you and even me. In the end, we're all the same… living a worthless pointless life, just waiting to die. I have been asked over and over again why… why did I do it? And I have given many answers… all different," Jason said.

"And what is the truth? Why did you do it?" Harvey asked.

"You know, I don't even know myself. Hahaha… Goodbye, Detectives. It's been fun. I will miss you," Jason said.

"Just get in the damn plane and never come back," James said.

"I wouldn't be so rude to me, Jim, or one day, I may just decide to come back. I may just visit your wife… your kids… and test if Amanda's hand is any stronger than the last time," Jason said.

James clenched his fist in rage. Jason looked into his soul and said, "It's good to know that no matter what I will always be in there (Jason tapped his head). I will always haunt you in your mind. You will wake at night screaming at the thought of me. I am the monster under your bed, and you don't forget ever. I… beat… you… and you will suffer for the rest of your pathetic life… all because of me."

Jason smiled and walked away from James and Harvey and held Jacob's and Izzy's hands as they entered the private plane. Jason sat down.

"Where are we going, daddy?" Jacob asked.

Jason looked out the window at Harvey and James and spoke, "A new beginning, son. We're headed to a new beginning."

Jason waved at Harvey and James. The plane took off.

"Let's go. Don't let him live in your mind, Jim. Come on, I'll buy you a beer," Harvey said.

"Yeah, yeah… Alright… time to forget…" James said.

They walked away.

Chapter 18

Harvey pulled up outside James's house with James in the passenger seat.

"Hey, Jim, are you sure you're alright?" Harvey asked.

"Of course, I finally get a night's rest. Why wouldn't I be alright?" James asked.

"Well, I know you told me to let him go, but I don't think you have. Well, Jim, have you let him go?" Harvey asked.

James paused before saying, "You know I don't think I can. I don't think I can, Harv. I don't know how to forget the things he's done: the people, Marcus, Cecil, Walker, Martin, George, and so many more… I can't forget."

"I know. Their faces will be with you forever, but you must try. Make the best of what you have. Go, go to your family, Jim, and try and move on," Harvey said.

"I'll try. Thank you, Harvey. You're more than a good friend. You are my brother," James said.

"You're my brother, too," Harvey replied.

"See you Monday," James replied. James climbed out of Harvey's car and walked into his house and called out, "I'm home, Amanda. You up?"

"Yeah, just putting Lenny to bed," she called down.

"Alright," James replied. James poured himself a glass of water and took some pills. He sighed and heard someone saying, "Hello, Jim."

James slowly reached for his gun. The voice said, "Don't I have one too?"

"What do you want?" James asked.

"Your help," the voice said.

"Help with what?" James asked.

"Turn around," the voice said.

James turned around and saw. It was Anthony.

"Anthony, you're alive? I thought…"

Anthony interrupted, "You thought he killed me too, just as he did my brother and father and everyone else. He tried. He made me watch as he burnt them and killed them. I saw everything… every minute detail of their deaths… their pain… their agony. I experienced it all."

"What do you want from me, Anthony?" James asked.

"I told you I want your help," Anthony said.

"With what?" James asked.

Anthony said angrily, "DON'T PLAY DUMB WITH ME. You know what I want. Where is he? I know you know. Tell me, James. Let me kill him. Let me end the suffering."

"I can't tell you," James said.

Anthony got and said, "He's already killed so many. He killed my father, my brother… and I know what he's done to you… kidnapped and tortured your wife… brutally butchered your friends and colleagues. Let me stop him Jim, so he can't take anymore from anyone else. Please let me avenge them all. I know you remember all of them… all their faces flashing through your mind. Let me stop it. Let me kill the monster."

"OK OK, Anthony, I'll help, but promise me... promise me..." James paused.

"Promise you what?" Anthony asked.

"Promise me... you'll make it hurt," James finished.

"Don't worry, I will make it agony," Anthony said.

"All I know is he was heading to Canada. It's a big place," James said.

"And I will search every inch of it looking for him. I've left my number on the side. Call me of any information you learn. Thank you. Goodbye, Jim," Anthony cut in.

James fell onto the couch.

Chapter 19

Five Years Later

Jason was lying in bed as a woman was doing her hair at a table.

"Well, look, who's up? Last night was great," she said.

Jason rose to his feet. "I'm much more excited for what comes next," he whispered.

"Oh, yeah, and what's that?" the woman asked.

Jason wrapped his belt around her neck and strangled her. She struggled and failed.

"Huh, déjà vu," Jason said.

Eventually, she stopped.

Jason said to her corpse, "Ahh… never gets old."

While trying to leave, Jason heard a cry from an adjacent room. He entered and saw a small child sitting on the floor. They stared at each other. As the child was crying, Jason squatted down saying, "Hello there, little guy, it's OK. No need to cry… huh… you know my kids were just as small as you once, but that was a long, long time ago when I was legendary, and now I am a myth, how time flies.

"I still can't believe it's been five years since I left that life behind… left behind my magnum opus over 15 years of thorough planning all in the past. You should've seen it. It was beautiful… the look on their faces as I… as I made them suffer, but there were some, some who stood against me, showed no fear, but even they fell just like the rest. I wonder what you will grow to be. Only time will tell... huh... anyway, I've got to go. Goodbye."

Jason saw a small bottle of milk and said, "Oh, do you mind?" He drank it and said, "It keeps the mind active." Jason left.

Jason was at his new home. Jacob and Izzy were eating cereal.

"Morning, shouldn't you be dressed for school?" Jason asked.

"It's an off day," Jacob said.

"So it is," Jason replied.

"Where were you last night?" Izzy asked.

"Just work as always. Anyway, how was last night? Please tell me you didn't eat all the ice cream," Jason asked.

"Alright I won't tell you," Jacob said.

"Smart, just like I was," Jason chuckled.

James was at a party celebrating Harvey being promoted to captain. James and Harvey were in the captain's office.

"No, I can't do it," Harvey said.

"You're telling me you've been risking your life against criminals for the past... what... 80 years." James said.

"Hey," Harvey said.

James continued, "But you're afraid to give a speech."

"Yes. Alright... I'm scared to give the speech. What if I mess it up, and... and they all lose respect for me," Harvey said.

"You've worked with most of them for years. I doubt a stutter in your speech will change what they think of you," James said.

"Thanks, man," Harvey said.

"Because I don't see how they could see you any worse," James said.

Harvey looked annoyed. James said, "Sorry, sorry... I couldn't help myself. You're going to do great, Harv. I believe in you..."

Harvey stood up and took a deep breath. He took a swig of whiskey.

James said, "You sure that's going to help?"

"Hell, yeah... it will. (Deep breath!) OK, OK... let's go," Harvey said.

"You are sure you're ready?" James asked.

"No, but let's do it," Harvey said.

Harvey and James stepped out. James joined the others. Harvey took the stage. All the cops clapped and stood to listen to his speech.

"Thank you... thank you! As you all know, I'm Harvey, and I have worked as a cop for, god seems like a life time, and through all these years, I have seen things... some terrible things... and met some awful despicable people. However, how..."

He looked at James who encouraged him. Harvey gulped and continued, "However, I have also met some amazing people... all of you. You have all inspired me... inspired me to keep pushing and working hard. Well, you and also the increased pension."

The audience all chuckled. Harvey continued, "And now I have finally reached the title of captain, a rank when I first joined the force I never wanted, but one man motivated me to keep working in order to make our city and our people safer. And that man is Detective James."

James looked shocked not thinking this would happen as the audience all turned and looked at James. Harvey continued, "As you all know me and Detective James have been partners for, oh what is it like 15 years, and since the day I met him, I saw his heart... how much this job meant to him... how hard he worked... and it gave me a new look on my life, so tonight, we don't celebrate me... we celebrate Detective James."

Harvey began to clap. Everyone else clapped for James who looked stunned yet honoured. Harvey then said, "And last thing the bar is now open."

The audience cheered as they all dispersed back into the party. Harvey walked towards James.

"Now I know that wasn't in your original speech," James said.

"How could I leave you out? This is your honour, not mine," Harvey said.

"Don't be ridiculous, Harvey. You have put your blood, sweat and tears into this job and city and its people. This honour is all yours," James said.

"Very well, it's ours. How about that?" Harvey said.

"Alright ours," James said.

"Here's to us," Harvey said and grabbed two glasses from a waiter and handed one to James.

"To us," James said.

They drank the drink as James got a message on his phone reading, *Found him.*

James looked shocked as a sense of fear ran down his spine, and he spaced out until Harvey said, "Hey, hey, JAMES."

James snapped back into reality.

"What is it?" Harvey asked.

"Oh, nothing, excuse me for a moment. Would you?" James said. James walked away.

Harvey watched him in suspicion. James walked into a darkened office and called the number and said, "Come on, pick up... pick up..."

The phone was answered. James said, "Angela, are you being serious with me? Please tell me this isn't some practical joke."

"I'm being serious, James. 100%... we found him," Angela answered.

James looked stunned as he lost feeling in his legs. He grabbed the table to avoid falling down.

She asked, "James, are you alright?"

"Yea, yeah... I'm... I'm fine. Are... are you sure? Are you sure it's him?" James asked.

"I'm sure. The killings over the past couple weeks all match the data you sent me. I'm positive it's him. I'm sending you the information now. Get to a computer," Angela said.

James hurried over to a computer and logged on. He was emailed the recent killed victim.

"Yes, just like he has done before... same situation... same method... use of the fire alarm... it all matches. Oh, my god, I don't believe it. After all these years, I've finally got you," James said.

"How long have you been looking for him exactly?" Angela asked.

"Too long... too damn long..." James said.

"I've just sent you CCTV footage of the bar from last night, and do you see what I see?" Angela asked.

James looked over the footage. he saw him. He saw Jason.

"There you are… you son of a bitch. There's no running now," James said.

"The bartender said his name was George Peterson. I've done a search on our data base, and I found his address. I'm sending it to you now," Angela said.

James began to shed a tear.

"Thank you… thank you, Angela. He can finally pay for everything he's done. I don't know how to thank you as much as you deserve."

"You can thank me by killing the bastard. Goodbye, Jim. Hopefully, next, we talk it's toasting the monster's death," Angela said.

"Wait one more thing… I never asked why did you agree to help me. Why did you agree all those years ago to help me track him down, and not arrest him? Why?" James said.

"Are you sure you want to know?" Angela asked.

"Yes, I'm sure," James said.

"Do you remember, Sarah?" Angela asked.

"What Sarah are you talking about?" James asked.

Angela cut in, "The Sarah he strangled just like this girl. She is my sister, and after you called up and told me who you were looking for, I knew I couldn't let this monster live."

James looked sad, "I'm sorry. I don't know what to say," he said.

"Don't apologise. You didn't kill her. Just make sure the devil's dead," Angela said.

"I will… He's not escaping me again, not this time," James said.

"Goodbye, Jim. Speak to you later," Angela said.

"Goodbye," James said and hung up the phone.

A voice spoke from the shadow, "Who was that, Jim?"

James grabbed his gun and aimed it forward. But it was Harvey. James looked ashamed. He lowered the gun.

Harvey asked more angrily, "WHO WAS THAT?"

"How… how much did you hear?" James asked.

"Why should I tell you? So you can bend the truth? Who was it, Jim?" Harvey asked.

"Her name is… is Angela," James said.

"And who is Angela exactly?" Harvey asked.

"She's a cop in Canada," James said.

"I should've have known. I should have known you couldn't. You wouldn't let him go even after you told me to. A part of me knew that deep down, you were still holding on. Even after all these years, every time he is brought up and mentioned, you shrink… you get angry… you try to hide it… and you do hide it from a lot of people, but not from me," Harvey said.

"Look, Harv, I'm sor—" James said.

"Don't apologise to me. You know I'm not only hurt that you have kept obsessing over him for all these years but that you also hid it from me. WE FACED HIM TOGETHER, JIM… together, and you shut me out. WHY?" Harvey asked.

"Because I didn't want you to get hurt. I didn't want this on your mind," James said.

"And I told you I've already got so much on it already," Harvey said.

"Alright then, but if I had told you, would you be where you are now? Huh… would you be the honourable decorated and newly appointed captain you are today? The truth is you wouldn't," James said.

"How are you going to do it?" Harvey said.

"What?" James asked.

"Well, you've found him, so how are you going to do it. How are you going to do exactly what he wants you to do? Huh… you going to fly over there yourself? You going to get Angela to do it?" Harvey asked.

"No, none of that," James said.

"THEN HOW?" Harvey asked again.

"ANTHONY… Anthony Spire…" said James.

Harvey looked stunned and even more betrayed and said, "An… Anthony Spire? Anthony Spire's dead. He died in a building explosion set up by Jason Mitchell's."

James shook his head, "No, you're wrong. He escaped. He survived," he said.

"And how do you know that?" Harvey said.

"Because… because that night, the night that monster escaped while I stood there and watched him, Anthony came to me. He asked for my help, and so I agreed. Alright… YOU HAPPY, HARV? THAT'S HOW I'M GONNA DO IT. ANTHONY SPIRE IS GOING TO KILL THE BASTARD IN THE EXCRUCATING WAY THAT HE DESERVES," James said.

Harvey looked sick and said, "It's not too late you know."

"Not too late for what?" James asked.

"To delete the number, to move on, to let him go, to do the same thing you told me to do…" Harvey said.

James looked broken and said, "I… I… I can't, Harv. I can't move on. I can't let him go. You don't understand every waking moment of my life since that day has been filled with… with suffering. Even when I sleep, all I see is him coming back, coming for Amanda, for my children… for you… And I won't let that nightmare become a reality."

In despair, Harvey started walking away.

"Where are you going?" James asked.

"I'm too late. He's already done exactly what he said he would," Harvey said.

"What do you mean? Done what?" James asked.

Harvey said, "For such a good detective, you truly are blind by your hatred for him... your fear of him. He said that suffering is a cycle, and he was right, just like it did to him the day he killed Marcus. The suffering has consumed you as well."

James looked shocked.

Harvey continued, "He did exactly what he said he would. Even now he's still one step ahead moving us like puppets, so there's nothing I can do or say anymore, no matter what as soon as I leave. You're going to pick up that phone and tell Anthony Spire exactly where to find him, so why waste my breath. Goodbye, Jim. I hope one day you can learn to truly forgive yourself."

Harvey walked out as James sat there in complete silence, completely defeated and stunned.

"I'm sorry, Harvey, but he must die... he must pay... even if that is what he wants," he finally said. James picked up his phone and rang Anthony.

Anthony picked up. "Hello, Jim. It's been a while."

"So it has," James replied.

"How's Harvey and Amanda and little Lenny or how about little Helen?" Anthony asked.

"They're all good," James replied.

"And I heard you have another little one coming along, congratulations," Anthony replied.

"Thank you," James said.

"What news have you for me?" Anthony asked.

"I found him… I found him, Anthony," James said.

"Where?" Anthony asked in desperation.

"I'll message you a photo of the area," James responded.

"Finally, after all this time, he will burn, and my father and brother can rest. Thank you, Jim. I won't forget this," Anthony said.

"Anthony, before you go," James said.

"Yes, Jim," Anthony said.

"Make him suffer," James said.

Anthony chuckled.

"As if I wouldn't, he will suffer more than he knows is possible. Goodbye, Jim."

James fell back in the chair as the phone ended. He looked directly at his monitor, which had a zoomed in picture of Jason's face.

"This is the end. You will no longer haunt me. You've lost. No matter what Harvey said, you've lost, and I have won. I hope it burns. I hope you experience more pain than all of your victims combined," James said. "I hope you suffer."

Chapter 20

Anthony was in an office in his garage as he looked at a picture of his father and brother as he heard his father's last words repeating in his head slowly getting louder, "You'll burn for this. You'll burn for this. YOU'LL BURN FOR THIS. YOU'LL BURN FOR THIS."

"When?"

Anthony snapped himself out of it as he hallucinated seeing Jason.

Jason said, "That really was a good day, wasn't it?"

Anthony seemingly unfazed by this said, "Go away; not now."

"Oh, why not? I know you miss me," Jason said.

"Piss off," Anthony said.

"You see, I can't because I'm in your head. If you really didn't want me here, I wouldn't be here. (Jason got closer to Anthony.) Face it. You like the pain. You miss the misery I caused you," Jason said.

Anthony jumped forward and backed down Jason saying, "You're right. I do want you here because I want to look into your eyes one last time before I pull them from your skull, before I burn you. That's why you're here. Tell me, are you ready to face the consequences of your actions?"

Jason acted defeated when he laughed.

Anthony looked confused and said, "What's so damn funny?"

"You tell me, you're the one making me laugh." Jason said.

Anthony grabbed Jason and shook him screaming, "NO… NO… I'M NOT."

Jason still laughing said, "You're afraid. Hahaha… you're terrified of me."

"No, you're wrong… you're lying…" Anthony said.

Jason continued, "I live in your head, Anthony, and I have done so for the past five years. Face it. You don't know how to live without me… hahahaha…"

Anthony began to lose it and said, "Shut the hell up."

"You're happy that I killed your father and brother, aren't you? I bet, if they were still here, you'd let me kill them, wouldn't ya?" Jason asked.

Anthony completely lost it and pulled out his knife and stabbed Jason again and again and again until someone entered his office and said, "Boss… boss… BOSS…" Anthony snapped out of it.

"Wha… yes, what is it?"

"I heard yelling. Are you OK, boss?" the thug asked.

Anthony looked back to where Jason was but only saw a chair with several stab marks on it. He paused before saying, "Yeah… yeah, I'm good because today is the day."

"What did you find him, boss?" the thug asked.

"Oh, I found him alright. Gather the others… go," Anthony said.

The thug rushed out and yelled at others.

Anthony looked at the photo of his family once more and said in sadness nearly crying, "He will burn, father. You have

147

waited all these years so patient, but today is the day. I will avenge you. I will show him the pain you swore upon him with your final breath. Don't worry, he will die no matter what."

Anthony walked out onto a balcony overlooking dozens of armed thugs as they all stood at attention. He wiped the tears going in his eyes and said, "We have fought long and hard… five years to be exact, and finally, the day has arrived. Today, we kill JASON MITCHELLS."

The thugs cheered as Anthony continued, "HE HAS TAKEN… HE HAS RIPPED AWAY SO MUCH FROM US, AND NOW HE WILL PAY FOR EVERYTHING. TOGHTHER WE WILL AVENGE EVERYONE HE HAS TAKEN AND MAKE SURE HE NEVER TAKES ANYTHING ELSE FROM ANYONE. ARE YOU WITH ME?"

They all cheered again as Anthony nodded his head and raised his hand yelling, "LET THE DEVIL BURN."

They all cheered once again and yelled repeating again and again.

"LET THE DEVIL BURN. LET THE DEVIL BURN. LET THE DEVIL BURN."

Anthony basked in it for a moment before saying, "Then let's go do it."

They all rushed around and began to prepare as Anthony looked into the distance and said to himself, "No more running… no more hiding… no more killing… Today is the last day you breathe. Tonight, you will know true suffering. I hope you're ready." Anthony walked away.

It was night. Jason's house was in darkness. He was watching a movie with Jacob and Izzy, all laughing together. His phone buzzed. He checked it and stood up.

"Where are you going?" Izzy asked.

"I just got to take this for a moment," Jason responded.

"Should we pause it for you?" Jacob asked.

"No no. Keep it going. I'll only be a minute," Jason said and walked into the kitchen. His phone rang. He picked it up and said, "Hello."

A voice responded, "Hello, Jason. It's been a while."

"Who is this?" Jason asked.

"Let me give you a hint. You will BURN," the voice said.

Jason looked shocked and said, "Anthony?"

"Yes. Oh, it's been so long since you said my name. I bet you didn't expect to be hearing from me." Anthony laughed.

"I'm impressed. Not only did you survive, but after all these years, you haven't stopped searching. Tell me how you did it. How did you find me?" Jason asked.

"From a neutral friend," Anthony said.

Jason chuckled and spoke, "Jim?"

"Tell me, how does it feel to know that you've lost… that everything you've done has come back to haunt you?" Anthony said.

Jason laughed.

Anthony asked, "Why are you laughing?"

"Why don't you tell me how it feels?" Jason asked.

"How what feels?" Anthony asked.

"How does it feel to have me live inside of your head for five years? What have I been doing to you and Jim all this time?" Jason asked.

"I don't care," Anthony said.

"How far away are you?" Jason asked.

"I'm right here," Anthony said. The phone hung up.

Jason's phone read security breach. He opened the video and saw over a dozen armed men. Bang... they fired through the windows destroying the house. One bullet fired through Jason's shoulder. Jason ignored the pain as he dived on Izzy and Jacob being shot in the stomach. Doing so, he then pulled out a handgun from under the couch and fired out the porch window killing one attacker.

"What's happening?" Izzy screamed. Jason grabbed both of their hands and sprinted into the basement.

"What are you doing? Oh my god, you're bleeding," Jacob said panicked.

Jason pushed over a bookcase revealing a hidden tunnel. "Go... follow the tunnel. It will take you to safety. Go... I'll hold them off," Jason said.

"No, we won't leave you," Jacob said.

Jason smirked holding them daringly.

"I won't make it, son. Here's the location of my hidden money a few million. Now go... live... live a different life."

"Are you coming too?" Izzy asked.

"No, this is where my story ends. But you go and live your own," Jason said. They leaped on him hugging him, "We love you, dad."

Jason paused before hugging them back saying, "I love you, too."

They ran out the tunnel as Jason barricaded it behind him. He held his wound as blood poured from it.

"Time to end this," he said. He ran up the stairs and opened a secret panel revealing an assault rifle, monitors and buttons. He watched the monitors. He pushed one button in the dining room where two attackers were. A painting fell revealing a wall of machine guns, which all fired killing the two men ripping them to shreds.

Then he pushed another button. In the front garden, one attacker approached the house. As he stepped on the door mat, it held for a moment before opening dropping the attacker into a pit of spikes.

Gun fire hit the wall next to him. Jason quickly pressed another button and leaped out the way as multiple pieces of the walls open and fire spiked out killing four attackers impaling them to the walls of the house. Jason rose again. He was shot in the leg. He rolled to the side and popped the attacker in the head. When two more entered a different way, Jason popped one, then dived over the coffee table dodging past gun fire before popping the other upon landing.

"Is that all you got? COME ON, SHOW ME YOUR VENGEANCE. SHOW ME," Jason yelled. When he was shot in the back, he spun round and fired several shots hitting the attacker twice in the chest and once in the head.

Jason walked into the dining room, but when he went round the corner, he was tackled into a wall. The attacker stabbed Jason in the gut. Jason took the pain headbutting the attacker, then kicking him back. Jason ripped out the knife from his own stomach, throwing it to his left hitting another attacker in the eye. Jason then punched the attacker several times before grabbing his head and shoving his thumbs through his eyes. The attacker yelled in agony. Jason started bashing the attacker's skull against the wall turning it to mush.

Jason then pulled a handgun from the attackers pocket and fired at several others killing three, but they shot back, hitting him in the legs, the chest and the mouth. Jason fell back as the attackers surrounded him. Jason acted defeated when one stood directly above him.

"Please, oh, please have mercy," Jason said. Jason then pulled out a knife from his shoe and impaled the attacker in the bottom of the throat as the other attackers unloaded into Jason, ripping into him. Jason fully collapsed to the ground as blood flooded from him. Anthony entered and said, "Hello, Jason. It's been a while," Anthony said.

Jason laughed, "Hahahahaha… ahhh… that it has. Anthony, you know I still see them… your father and brother screaming in agony as I—"

Bang… Anthony shot Jason in the leg.

"SHUT UP… DON'T YOU SAY THEIR NAMES. DON'T YOU MENTION THEM," Anthony shouted.

"Ouch (coughing)… ah… I envy you, Anthony. I killed your family for you. I set you free. I had to do that myself with mine. Hahaha…" Jason coughed.

"You deserve all of this… all of this pain and agony… you're worse than a monster," Anthony said.

"Good… now you see it. This is our story, Anthony. A tale of two villains, just like everything… every book… every god damn movie… In every story, there is no hero only the winner, and the winner tells us that he was the hero, but if the roles were reversed, the other guy would say the same thing. What are you waiting for, hero? Exact your revenge," Jason replied.

"No, I want to savour the moment. We all do, or haven't you figured it out yet? Jason, we are all here because of you. Every single one of us is here because you took something from us. So tell me, Jason, how does it feel knowing you caused all of this, you killed yourself?"

Jason paused and then said, "It makes me feel… victorious."

Anthony looked confused, "Now look who doesn't see it. You think my plan ended with the death of your father. No… no… no… you could not be more wrong. This is the ending of my plan. The cycle of suffering continues," Jason said.

"What…? What are you talking about?" Anthony asked.

"The principle… suffering is a disease. It spreads. It started with my bully Marcus's father. He abused him. He made him suffer, and then Marcus made me suffer, so I killed him and made so… so many suffer… you… Jim… all of my victims… and you are now completing the cycle killing the one who made you suffer, just like I did to Marcus. And I'm sure he would have killed his father if he had the chance. Now you finally know WHY? Why I did it all? Because you all needed to suffer… all this time, and you've still been doing exactly as I wanted. I only thought it would be Jim here instead of you, but one mistake. But the results are the same. Kill me and complete the cycle. Enjoy MY DEATH… MY SUFFERING… MAKE ME BURN JUST AS YOUR FATHER WANTED," Jason said (coughing blood).

Anthony hesitated before saying, "I will. And now you will burn like my father. You will suffer. Goodbye, Jason," Anthony shot Jason several times in the chest while his men set fire to the house. Anthony left with his men.

Jason's blooded face was still his mind and had a single thought, "So… this… this is what it feels like."

Jason's eyes remained open as the fire consumed him, and his life faded from him. People watched as the fire engulfed the house and his body. Jason burns for his sins. The house collapsed on top of him.

Outside, one of Anthony's men said, "Should we go after the kids?"

"No, they have nothing to do with this. The monster is dead. It's all over," Anthony responded. Anthony continued to watch the fire and said, "I did it, father. You can now rest."

The house started collapsing in on itself. Anthony continued to watch with pure contentment. Jason burnt to a crisp and was buried under the rubble of his despair.

Chapter 21

James and Harvey were watching the newsreader.

"Jason Mitchells, revealed to have been living in Canada under the name George Peterson also known as the infamous serial killer, the Reaper, is dead. He was brutally shot and burnt last night. Officials have no suspect at the moment as Officer Angela Kelly had this to say."

James smiled, "How do you feel? You got what you wanted? He's gone," Harvey said.

"Look, I'm sorry, Harvey. I'm sorry for everything… for lying to you… for hiding this from you for years. I just didn't want you to have to bear with any more than you already did. I swear on my life I will never lie to you again. Please forgive me," James said.

"Thank you, but don't you ever lie to me again. If I want to help you, I will. You're more than my partner, James… you are my brother," Harvey said.

James smiled and said, "You're my brother, too, Harv."

Harvey and James hugged.

"So, tell me, how do you really feel?" Harvey asked.

"I… I don't know. A part of me is happy released," James said.

"And the other?" Harvey asked.

"I'm not sure. It just doesn't feel right," James said.

Suddenly, James got a message on his phone. He looked at it.

"Who is it?" Harvey asked.

"Anthony," James said.

Anthony was kneeling in front of his father and brothers graves and placed down a glass of champagne for each of them. He looked depressed and said, "You two should celebrate. You've done it. You're at peace, but not me. I will never be at peace. I will be haunted by him for the rest of my life… cheers."

Anthony downed his glass as James and Harvey arrived. They walked towards him.

Harvey said, "What is he doing here? If anyone sees him?"

"Let's find out," James said.

"Anthony, what are you doing here? If anyone sees you, you'll be arrested? You can't be here," James asked.

"I know. That's why I'm here," Anthony answered.

"What are you talking about?" Harvey asked.

"He won, Jim," Anthony said.

"What? Who won?" James asked.

"He did. Jason; we both played into his hands," Anthony said.

"If that were true, he'd still be alive," Harvey said.

"No, you don't understand. He wanted me to kill him. He told me. He told me that suffering. It's a cycle. It started with some kid named Marcus's father, and then it spread to Marcus and then him… and now us… He proved his point. The cycle continues. He continues," Anthony said.

"No, don't let him get in your head," James said.

"He's been in my head for five years, and I know he's been in yours a hell of a lot longer. He isn't truly dead, Jim. He's still in here. He lives on in me," Anthony said. Anthony pointed to his head and continued, "I can still feel him... see him. He haunts me."

"But now he's gone. You have avenged your family and stopped a mad man. You're a hero. You beat him," James said.

"I'm no hero, Jim. I've done things... terrible things, and I want to pay for them. I don't want the hate and the suffering to consume me like it did to him all these years of hunting Jason. It has been like a pilgrimage. It has been enlightening, and I'm ready to let the suffering die with me," Anthony said.

"Are you sure? You can leave now. Never look back and start a new life try and overcome the suffering," James asked.

"There is no overcoming it, only locking it away. I'm not as strong as you, Jim. I can't fight it," Anthony said.

"Are sure about this? There's no going back," Harvey said.

"I'm sure. Maybe after a life of suffering, I can rest in death," Anthony said.

Harvey put hand cuffs around Anthony and spoke, "You're a good man, Anthony. I'm sorry it had to end like this."

"It's not that bad. It's not that bad," Anthony said.

"Anthony, would you honour me with being the namesake of my new-born son," James said.

"I would be honoured, Jim, but save that for a man who deserves it," Anthony said.

"Come on, I'll buy you a beer on the way," Harvey said as they walked away.

A man is truly lost once suffering has consumed him!